"Brilliantly prepared and exquisitely presented . . . a story of immense wisdom whose main ingredient is love. And by the way, if you find your eyes watering at the end—it isn't the onions."

— Bob Burg, coauthor, *The Go-Giver* and *The Go-Giver Leader*

"A blueprint for transcending limitations and living a big life. *The Recipe* will speak directly to your heart and help you find your way."

— Michael Port, author, *Book Yourself Solid* and *The Think Big Manifesto*

"A coming-of-age story, a meditation on food and the art of cooking, and a life manual, all wrapped together into one exquisite package. Carroll and Mann have crafted a tale of struggle and triumph that touched my heart and inspired my soul. *The Recipe* is magical."

— Lisa Earle McLeod, author, *Leading with Noble Purpose*

"A delicious read in more ways than one: descriptions of food so vivid your taste buds tingle—and a great story to warm your heart."

— Robert G. Allen, author, *Multiple Streams of Income*

"Cooking is like life: if you don't pay attention to the small things, the day-to-day slicing and dicing, the larger presentation can become an absolute mess. *The Recipe* is a great instrument for sharpening your knife."

— Josh Ellis, editor in chief, *SUCCESS* magazine

"*The Recipe*: one part motivational fable, one part human drama, one part coming of age, one part how-to book; add a dash of mystery, a drop of conspiracy, sprinkle liberally with wisdom, nobility, and humor, and—*voilà*—you've got the feel-good book of the year!"

— James Justice, screenwriter, *Primal Rage* and *Lesser Evil*

"Every business leader should give a copy of this book to their staff, and every parent should give it to their children. *The Recipe* will be my Christmas gift to friends and family this season."

— Linda K. Carroll, CCM, past president, Club Managers of America

"Carroll and Mann have done a fantastic job paralleling the joys and challenges of cooking to those we face in life. The story will draw you in, and chefs and home cooks alike will learn from these lessons of the kitchen."

— Chef John Folse, host, PBS's *After the Hunt*

"Into this wonderfully crafted and engaging story, the authors have interwoven the ingredients for long-lasting personal and professional success with lessons of leadership, mentorship, patience, love, passion, and endurance. The recipes in the back are worth the price of the book. Enjoy and savor!"

— David Cottrell, author, *Monday Morning Leadership*

"Eloquent, heartfelt, honest, and wise . . . You will feel the passion, commitment, and dedication to process on every page."
— Chef Kirk T. Bachmann, M.Ed., campus president, Escoffier School of Culinary Arts

"A wonderful and compelling story . . . Owen's journey is one of growth, maturation, and the cultivation of integrity and a strong work ethic—values that go well beyond the culinary profession and apply to all of life."
— James E. Griffin, Ed.D., CEC, CCE, associate professor, Johnson & Wales University

"What a charming story . . . The boy Owen and the old chef both won my heart—and I became a better cook in the process!"
— Joanne King Herring, Consulate General of Pakistan and Morocco,
Medal of Honor nominee, subject (the Julia Roberts character)
of the 2007 Mike Nichols film *Charlie Wilson's War*

"A fascinating collection of time-tested cooking principles embedded into a delightful story. The authors' commonsense approach, both to cooking and to life experience, makes this book a valuable addition to anyone's library."
— Chef Ferdinand Metz, CMC, AAC, president emeritus, Culinary Institute of America,
past president, American Culinary Federation

"Transformative! *The Recipe* helps you see the foundation to build a life you love."
— Dave Fuehrer, adjunct professor, Rochester Institute of Technology,
young adult cancer survivor

"*The Recipe* is a young culinary professional's guide for managing yourself in an industry that demands excellence in everything we do."
— Chef Tom Vaccaro, CEPC, dean, School of Baking and Pastry,
Culinary Institute of America

"Teen readers will identify with Owen's struggles and come away with new optimism and hope for a life of adventure and success. The adult reader will find a poignant narrative with abundant practical lessons. As an educator and a coach for nearly four decades, I can't wait to make *The Recipe* part of our curriculum."
— Randy Stelter, Wheeler High School-Union Township
Middle School, Valparaiso, Indiana

"A wonderfully engaging and inspiring story with insights that will make you a better person—and recipes that will delight the amateur chef in all of us! *The Recipe* is my favorite book this year."
— Jeff C. West, leadership coach, author, *The Unexpected Tour Guide*

"Read this book! You'll love the principles and appreciate the wisdom."
— Nido Qubein, president, High Point University

the recipe

AUSTIN
DAVID
BOOKS

the recipe

a story of loss, love, and
the ingredients of greatness

chef charles carroll
john david mann

AUSTIN DAVID BOOKS

Austin David Books
Amherst, Massachusetts
austindavidbooks.com

ISBN 978-0-9988626-0-6
Library of Congress Control number: 2017939991
Printed in the United States of America

Cover art by Hannah Ineson
Set in Fairfield and Adobe Caslon Pro

For Torill and Ana

contents

1

the diner

The wind whipped at Owen's jacket as he trudged up the long slate steps. When he reached the old diner's front entrance he stopped and turned, putting his back to the door and facing into the bitter February blast.

He tried not to look, but he couldn't help himself.

There it stood, across the street, dark and deserted, its brick-work looming four stories, long rows of windows glaring back at him. He shivered. One of the big warehouse windows was sealed over with cardboard and duct tape.

Vandalism.

The night before, he'd overheard his mom talking quietly on the phone in the next room. He knew it was about him, but all he'd caught was the word "reparation." He'd had to look it up. *The making of amends for a wrongdoing by paying money or other compensation.* That had sent him off to sleep feeling even worse.

He heaved a big breath and the shivers stopped.

"This is stupid," he muttered.

He turned back and pushed the door open. Snowflakes spiraled around his feet, following him as he stepped inside and shut the diner door behind him.

The place was simple, brightly lit, gleaming clean.

"Hello?" he called out as he looked around. Six booths lined the windows on his left, facing the side street; to his right, a long counter lined with a dozen old-fashioned pedestal stools. Three small tables punctuated the center aisle. Owen tried to picture how many people would fill this space. Forty, fifty maybe? Right now, at four thirty on a Friday afternoon, there was not a soul in the place.

Chopchopchopchopchop. . . .

The sound startled him. Glancing off to his right, he found its source: a grizzled old guy, just visible through a pass-through in the wall behind the counter, focused on his chopping block.

"Hello?" Owen repeated, as he took a few steps toward the pass-through. The man stopped what he was doing and looked up. "I . . . I need to speak with the owner?"

The man set his knife down, wiped his hands on a small towel hanging at his waist, and peered through the opening at the boy. Owen couldn't read the expression on his face.

"You the boy here about some work." More a statement than a question.

Owen nodded.

"Right," said the man. He disappeared for a moment, then emerged through a set of swinging doors at the end of the counter and walked up the aisle toward Owen. "Let's see what you can do."

"Excuse me?"

"You like to cook?" the man said.

Owen shrugged. "I guess."

The truth was, Owen *loved* to cook. In his fourteen years on earth, some of his happiest times had been cooking and eating with his parents, and he was drawn to the kitchen almost as much as he was to the baseball diamond.

At least, he used to be. These days he wasn't really drawn to much of anything. Getting into fights, maybe.

"Have a seat," said the man, nodding at the nearest stool. "Let's see what you can do."

"Wait. This is a test?" Owen felt his cheeks burn. "Like an audition?"

The man said nothing, just looked at Owen.

"The thing is," said Owen, "they told me I *had* to come work here. On weekends, to pay for . . ." Owen paused, and his cheeks burned hotter.

"The thing is," he repeated, "your boss, the guy who owns this place? I owe him some money. So they said I could maybe work here, on weekends. To pay him back, basically. Didn't they tell you all this?"

The man nodded. "That they did. Doesn't mean I have to agree. If you're gonna cook at my grill I need to know who I'm dealing with here."

Owen felt like punching something. Coming here to face the owner was hard enough in the first place. And now he was haggling with the *cook*?

"Um, shouldn't I talk with the owner? They told me to come talk with the owner."

The cook shrugged. "I'm who's here right now. You can talk to me."

Owen heaved a sigh. "Okay," he said. "What's the test?"

"Two parts," said the cook. "First comes eating."

"I don't understand. You want to know if I know how to *eat*?"

"Sit." The cook gestured again at the stool and headed back through the swinging doors into the kitchen. Owen heard the hiss of something hitting hot steel. An instant later his nostrils confirmed the sound of something savory on the grill—and an instant after that his stomach reminded him that he hadn't eaten since that morning. It had been a long day.

It felt like the last six months had been one long day.

No, he corrected himself, *not six months*. In fact it was exactly four months, three weeks, and two days since that terrible moment . . . sitting in class on a perfectly ordinary September day, when someone from the main office had come to the classroom door right in the middle of third-period History, knocked quietly, and—

Owen stopped himself from following the thread of that memory any further, and instead forced his attention onto the cook, who was just then emerging through those swinging doors again.

"This is stupid," he repeated under his breath as he took his seat at the counter.

The cook walked up behind the counter to where Owen sat and set a plate in front of him, then followed it with a glass filled with dark liquid shot through with bubbles fizzing up to the surface.

Owen looked at it in disbelief.

"A hot dog and a Coke? That's the big culinary test?" This was bogus. Owen was tempted to get up and walk back out the door.

Except that he couldn't, and he knew it. This had been the deal. Come to work at the diner, or be expelled—and even if he didn't especially care one way or the other, he couldn't do that to Mom. Not on top of everything else.

Okay, he'd humor the short-order cook. At least until the owner showed up.

The cook pushed over a second plate and glass, then came out from behind the counter, walked around behind Owen, and sat down at the next stool.

"A hot dog and a Coke," repeated Owen. "Very high class."

"Eat," said the cook.

Owen took a bite of his hot dog. The cook took a bite of his. They sat in silence for a minute, munching, Owen thinking, *A hot dog and a Coke. He wants to know if I know how to eat a hot dog and a Coke.*

"So," the cook broke the silence, "what do you think?"

"What do I think?" said Owen. "It's a hot dog." He didn't mean that to come out as rude as it sounded. But what was he supposed to say?

The cook nodded, then said, "How does it taste?"

Owen had been too wrapped up in his thoughts to notice how the thing tasted, but now that the man mentioned it . . . "It's pretty good," he admitted.

"Pretty good, how?" said the cook.

Owen stopped chewing and thought.

Pretty good . . . *how?*

He swallowed the bite and took another, trying to pay more attention to what he was eating. "It's . . . juicy. But not, I don't know, soggy?"

The cook said nothing, just waited.

Owen took another bite, tasting as he ate. "And meaty. Like it's . . . is there bacon in there?"

Owen saw something shift slightly in the cook's face, a change so faint he almost missed it. Was that a smile in his eyes? No, it must have been a trick of the light. This guy's face was flat as the winter sky.

"Not bacon," the cook was saying. "What you're tasting is an effect of the grill. Some places keep their hot dogs sitting in a tub of hot water so they'll be ready to go anytime. A lot of places do that. Not here. This one," he nodded at Owen's plate, "was sliced and cooked on the hot grill, hot enough and just long enough to slightly caramelize the surface. Which brings out its meatiness and gives it that savory edge—what you thought might be bacon. And also seals in the moisture. That's why it's not, as you put it, *soggy*.

"What else?"

Owen took another bite, trying to sharpen his sense of taste but not knowing exactly how to go about doing that. "Spicy, too, I guess." He thought some more. "But not *too* spicy."

"Spicy, how?"

Owen stopped chewing. Spicy, *how*? He tried as hard as he could to sort through what he was tasting and pick out the threads of flavor. He could sense them, but couldn't quite separate or identify them.

He looked at the cook. "I don't know. Pepper? Mustard?"

The cook was working on his own hot dog, and for a moment he didn't say anything, just kept chewing. Then he said, "Salt and pepper, 'course. White pepper, in this case. What else?"

Owen took another bite, frowning hard with concentration.

"Don't *think*," said the cook. "Don't try to guess what's in it. Tell me what it *tastes* like. How it feels on your tongue. How it makes you feel when you eat it."

"I guess," said Owen, "I guess I'd say it tastes . . . *really good*." He struggled to put it into words, but the best he could come up with was: "Like home."

The cook put his hot dog down, looked sideways at Owen, and nodded thoughtfully, as if the boy had made a deep observation.

"Garlic powder, just a little. Coriander. But my favorite? The celery seed. That's what you're tasting. That grassy, earthy taste. Makes it feel *like home*.

"And here's the other reason you thought of bacon—that

smoky taste? Hickory's what folks most often use. Mesquite's a big thing these days. Some swear by the fruit woods—apple, cherry, pear, like that. But this?" He closed his eyes and inhaled, as if he were tasting the hot dog all over again, then opened his eyes again. "Maple. Not so much smoke as you'd taste it, like the house next door burned down. A little smoky, a little sweet. Yeah," he nodded, as if cautiously agreeing with what he'd just said. "There's no taste more New England than maple."

Now that he mentioned it, Owen *could* taste that maple smoke, or at least he thought he could. But it would feel lame to say so now, after the cook had already explained it.

"Go ahead," said the cook, and he nodded at Owen's plate, which still had a scrap of hot dog left. "You don't want to leave any of that behind, do ya?"

"I don't," admitted Owen, as he dug in. "It's really good," he repeated. "*Better* than really good." In fact, he thought this might have been the best hot dog he'd ever had.

Or at least, that he'd had in a long time.

He closed his eyes and inhaled, like the cook had done, to better savor that last bite—and as he did, a vivid memory came over him:

the tangy scent of a summer evening in a stadium packed with people . . . the smell of hot dogs grilling and popcorn popping and peanuts roasting in their shells . . . the crack! *of a bat and sudden swell of the crowd's roar around him as they all leapt to their feet, and him with them . . . the wonderfully comfortable weight of his father's big hand on his back . . .*

His father's hand.

He stopped chewing. Opened his eyes. This wasn't summer, it

was February, and it was bitter cold outside.

"Yup," said the cook quietly, as if he'd been reading Owen's thoughts. "Good food calls up good memories. Reminds you of good times you've had, people you love."

Owen struggled to get his feelings under control. He listened to his own breathing, the way his father had taught him to do on the pitcher's mound to steady himself.

The cook wiped his mouth with a paper napkin, folded it into thirds, dropped it on the plate, and got up off the stool before continuing.

"Owen," he said, "I could sit you down to a five-course, two-hundred-dollar spread, serve myself a hot dog and a Coke, and you know which one of us would end up having the better meal?"

Owen figured that had to be a trick question, though he didn't really get how. "You would?"

"I would," the cook agreed. "You know why?"

Owen shook his head. "No idea."

Wait—had the cook just called Owen by name? Had he *told* him his name? He didn't think so.

"Because I've taught myself to *taste*," said the cook. "To put aside my thoughts, expectations, and judgments. To get myself out of the way, and experience what I'm experiencing.

"Great cooking is first in the eater. *Then* in the cook."

All at once Owen felt angry and confused. Why was this guy standing here talking to him about *great cooking*? Wasn't he just supposed to be here for a job? A job he didn't even want in the first place, but that he was being forced to take to get himself out of trouble and pay back the guy who owned this place?

Oh.

Owen looked up at the cook. "*You're* the owner. The chef."

The short-order cook nodded gravely. "That I am, Owen. That I am."

Now Owen felt even more confused. "So all those spices, the maple smoke and everything, was I supposed to taste all that? Did I just flunk?"

A pair of customers walked in the front door and stamped snow off their boots. The cook—no, the *Chef* glanced up at the wall clock over the door.

"Bernie'll be with you in a sec," the Chef called over to the two as they hung their coats on hooks by the door, and he started back toward the kitchen.

"Hang on, though," said Owen. "Didn't you say there were two parts? 'First comes eating.' What's the second part of the test?"

The Chef paused at the swinging doors and looked back at the boy. "Tell you what," he said. "Come back tomorrow morning. Oh eight hundred.

"Tomorrow you cook."

When Owen arrived home the house was dark. Mom wasn't home yet. He went into the kitchen, flipped on the lights, and started pulling things from the fridge. Tired as he was, he knew she'd be even more so. No problem. Sausages, scrambled eggs, toast: one-two-three.

Once he had the beaten eggs in a bowl and sausages sizzling on the stove, he put out two cloth napkins and set up two candles in holders. He brought out a single flower he'd picked up at the convenience store on his way home—a rose—and placed it in the center of the table in a one-stem vase.

When he heard his mom's car in the drive, he pushed down

the toast, then lit the candles, the sulfur smell of the match greeting her as she came through the front door in a blast of cold air.

"Tell me *everything*," she said, as she shucked off her parka and peeled out of her boots. "Did you go?"

Owen could hear how carefully she was keeping her voice neutral, and it made his chest hurt. She'd been worried he would back out, and not even show up at the diner.

"I did," he said. "I talked with the guy who cooks there. Turns out he's the owner."

"Ah, *ha*," she said. She gave Owen a long hug and planted a kiss on the top of his head. "And how was that?"

As they ate, Owen told her about his brief visit to the diner, about the hot dog and Coke, and about how the Chef had said, *Great cooking is first in the eater.*

"Sounds deep," she said. She puckered her lips and opened her eyes wide—what Owen's father always called "Beth's guppy stare" and always made them both crack up. Owen gave back a grin.

Beth got up from her chair, came around the table, and put her arms around her boy, resting her cheek on the top of his head.

"We'll get through this, honey," she murmured. "You're doing so great."

Was he? He didn't see how.

Later that night, after a fruitless hour or two of trying to engage his brain on homework, Owen lay awake in his bed, staring at his bedroom ceiling, thinking.

Tomorrow you cook, the cook had said.

No, he corrected himself, *not the cook. The* Chef.

Whatever test he might be walking into the next morning, he was determined not just to pass it, but to pass it with flying colors.

He owed it to Mom. For that matter, he wanted to show those people from school that he wasn't a total failure. Maybe he wanted to prove that to himself, too.

He closed his eyes.

Mostly, he just wanted to stop hurting.

2

the test

When he stepped into the diner the following morning at eight o'clock sharp, Owen almost didn't recognize the place. In the empty quiet of late afternoon the day before he'd thought they could seat forty or fifty, tops. Now it felt like there were eighty bodies jammed in there. Maybe a hundred. This place was buzzing like Times Square at rush hour.

Not that Owen had ever seen Times Square, or ever been out of Mapletown, for that matter. *I wish*, he thought.

A woman with RUTH stitched on her blouse pocket stood at the counter chatting with customers as she cleared their plates.

Owen took a seat at the counter's only open stool, the one closest to the door.

"Morning, Sunshine!" The woman was instantly there in front of him, placing a glass of water and handing him a menu.

"Uh, just some toast, ma'am. And maybe a hot chocolate?" He sure didn't feel like *morning sunshine*.

The day had not started out well. Owen was supposed to join his friends for ice hockey practice that morning. When they found out he wasn't coming because he had to go see a cook, they laughed at him. "Not just a cook, a *Chef*," Owen had protested, but that only made them laugh harder.

The truth was, he was nervous. Owen hated tests.

"Here ya go!" Ruth set his toast and hot chocolate down and disappeared again. Owen nibbled at the edge of his toast, waiting.

A moment later the Chef poked his head through the pass-through and called out, "Owen?" *Show time*. Owen got up from his stool, walked to the back of the diner, pushed through the swinging doors . . .

And stepped onto another planet.

The kitchen was tiny and cramped, packed with so much equipment that Owen could barely take it all in. A broiler, fryers, griddle, and bank of eight burners ran down one side of the long aisle, refrigeration units and prep stations along the other side. At the end of the corridor there stood a walk-in cooler and cold station, which he figured was where they made salads and sandwiches. Heavy stockpots hung by hooks over by the dishwasher and triple sink off to his left, and on the back corner of the stove he saw a stack of sauté pans that looked like they could be antiques—all bent and dinged up, none of them laying flat.

The place made Owen think of the galley on a pirate ship.

As he stood staring, a tall, rangy-looking guy (in his late twenties, Owen guessed) rushed around the place, his flame-red hair tied back in a bandana, hands and arms flying everywhere, tending what must have been six or seven different dishes at once. Standing at the burners he pivoted on one foot, yanked something out of the fridge, pivoted back with the fluid grace of a pro infielder and tossed it into the broiler with his right hand while snatching a hot sauté pan from the stack with his left.

And the noise! The screech and clang of oven doors opening

and closing, the sizzle of butter in the pans and bacon on the griddle, the *hissss!* of the spray hose hitting pots in the sink, the chugging of the massive industrial dishwasher that opened and closed like a guillotine, the *whooosh!* of steam when its door opened, and the constant din of dishes being picked up and put down, the metal plate covers clanging down to cover them, and the calls back and forth—"Need those waffles ay-sap!" "Order up!"—was enough to make Owen dizzy. And all this time that crazy breakfast cook kept mumbling to himself out loud.

The whole scene reminded Owen of the mad tea party in *Alice in Wonderland.*

The Chef, who seemed oblivious to the insanity going on around him, beckoned Owen over with a nod of his head and spoke a single word:

"*Station!*"

Owen wasn't sure what *Station!* meant, but he stepped over to the griddle, took the white apron the Chef handed him, and put it on.

"Ready?" said the Chef. "Two eggs, over easy. No meat, no toast, just spuds."

"Right," said Owen. As the only child in a hard-working two-income household, he'd done his share of breakfast duty, and eggs were his specialty. He could pull this one off with one hand tied behind his back. So this was the big test? *Bring it on.*

He grabbed a sauté pan from the stack with his left hand, spinning it one-handed by the handle (the way he'd watched chefs do it on TV) as he switched on the gas with his right hand and placed the pan on the burner. As the pan heated he quickly wrapped the apron strings around his waist and tied them in front.

Then he executed a perfectly coordinated two-hand maneuver: grabbing a sandwich-spreader with his right hand he scooped up a pat of butter and tossed it into the pan to sizzle, while he picked up an egg from the dozens sitting on the sideboard with his left, cracked it one-handed into the pan, tossed the shells, then grabbed a second egg and one-handed it in there to join its brother. While they cooked he stole a sideways glance to see if the Chef was watching.

He wasn't. He was out in front, chatting with a customer. Owen felt the knot tighten in his stomach and his cheeks burn.

Grabbing a spatula, he flipped first one egg, then the other. Moments later he had the two over easies on a plate, nestled up to a hot hillock of hash browns like a pair of puppies nuzzling their mother.

He tried not to let the grin of triumph show.

In the next instant the Chef was at Owen's side. He picked up Owen's plate with barely a glance, quietly set it aside on the back of the chopping-block counter, remade the order himself, and handed it off to Ruth without a word, then pulled the next ticket—a breakfast hash with two poached—and continued cooking.

Owen's plate sat.

Owen stood there, not knowing what to do. Was there something wrong with the plate he'd made? Was he dismissed?

As the Chef cooked he began talking. "Let me tell you the most important thing I ever learned from my teacher. *Everything you cook reveals everything you are.* If you're not focused, your food is going to be unfocused. If you're sloppy, your food will be sloppy. If you're in a hurry, the person who eats your food is eating a hurried up mess."

He looked over briefly, meeting Owen's eyes, as he said this next:

"If you're angry, you're going to cook angry."

While his eggs poached he pulled the next ticket. "Order French, pigs, no spuds!" he called over to the crazy mumbling cook.

"What's in here," he continued, thumping his chest with one hand as he pulled the next ticket with the other, "is what ends up on the plate."

He glanced at the ticket and started whisking eggs for an omelet.

"I don't understand," Owen began. "So . . . you didn't serve my eggs because you thought I was in a bad mood?"

The Chef glanced over at Owen. "I didn't serve them because they weren't any good." He saw the look on the boy's face and put his bowl of eggs down for a moment.

"It's a delicate thing, an over easy egg. You start with a decent sauté pan, ideally a non-stick pan. You heat the pan first, then put in the butter so it melts, and get the egg into the pan before the butter burns.

"The secret is how you manage the heat.

"Too little, and the egg sticks. Too much, and you start to denature the protein. It gets rubbery. If you start getting that crispy lip around the edge? You're losing the egg. Now you have to fight it to flip it, because it's not cooperating anymore, so now you have to use a spatula."

Owen winced. He'd used a spatula to get his eggs out of the pan. He'd gotten that crispy edge. He'd had the flame too high.

He'd been careless.

"If you've got it all in balance," the Chef was saying, "the egg will turn itself. All you have to do is give the pan a gentle flip with your wrist. You can practice that flip by putting a handful of dried peas in a cold sauté pan and flipping them until you can do it without any of them spilling out. Or beads. But it's not hard—not if you and the egg have gotten along up to that point."

Owen felt too mad to say anything. Mad at his hockey friends for being such jerks. At the Chef for giving him this stupid test. At himself for messing up again.

At the world.

The Chef spoke again as he slipped his finished omelet onto a plate.

"You may have had a bad morning, Owen. That's not your fault. You can't help that. But you can't serve your bad morning to someone else. Okay?"

Owen looked over at his eggs, sitting sullen at the back of the sideboard. They looked how he felt.

The Chef nodded over toward the pass-through, in the direction of Owen's abandoned plate of toast.

"Take five. The breakfast rush is almost over. We'll talk in a few minutes."

Owen pushed through the swinging doors, slunk back to his counter seat by the front door, and settled onto his stool. Next to his cold nibbled toast a fresh cup of hot chocolate sat sending up tendrils of steam. He caught a whiff of it—it smelled amazing, not like any hot chocolate he'd ever had before. *Spicy.*

"Just made," said Ruth.

"Thanks," mumbled Owen.

"He tell you, 'It's okay to make a mistake, just not okay to *serve* your mistake'?"

"Something like that," Owen admitted.

Ruth laughed as she collected her next round of used dishes with her right hand and stacked them all impossibly into her left arm. "I hope he's not keeping track, because when I started working for him—which was long before *you* were born—I served so many mistakes in my first week I started keeping a squeeze bottle of whiteout under the counter."

Owen could tell she was trying to buoy his mood, and even though it wasn't working, he appreciated it.

Ruth paused, her tower of dishes momentarily forgotten, and peered into his face. "You're Coach Devon's boy." More a statement than a question.

Owen nodded. "You knew my father?"

She looked at him for another moment, then gave him a smile that didn't hide its sadness. "A lot of people knew your father." She put out her right hand, the precarious stack of dishes at her left rattling slightly, yet remaining miraculously suspended in place. "I'm Ruth. And you must be—"

"*Owen!*" the Chef called out as he walked up the aisle toward them.

Owen looked up as the Chef took the stool next to him.

"You were good in there," said the Chef. "How you handled yourself. You knew your way around. That was clear."

Huh, thought Owen. So he *was* watching.

"And that spinning the pan thing? And the one-handed egg thing? Very impressive."

Owen blushed. He couldn't tell if the Chef was poking fun at him or really meant it.

"Here's the thing," said the Chef. "Cooking is about harnessing heat. Heat can burn, or it can build. You get to choose which. But it takes care, and attention.

"A chunk of life—an egg, for instance—can withstand even high heat for a time, use it to its advantage, help it transform into something else, a better version of itself. But heat is like a wild animal. If you don't temper it, wrangle it, it'll just wreak havoc, and that chunk of life ends up burnt, denatured, bitter.

"How you harness that heat. That's the important thing.

"You understand?"

Owen nodded uncertainly. *A chunk of life.* He'd never heard any food called *that* before. But he wasn't sure they were still talking only about food. *Burnt, denatured, bitter.* That about summed it up. That's pretty much how Owen felt these days.

Why couldn't things just go back to the way they were? He wanted his old life back. He wanted to be a happy kid again, a kid who didn't know anything about all this pain and confusion.

He wanted his father back.

Owen realized that the Chef was on his feet again, heading back to the kitchen.

"Wait," Owen called out. "So, did I pass?"

"Pass?"

"The test."

The Chef looked at Owen.

"The *test*. You said the test had two parts. 'First comes eating,' you said. 'Tomorrow you cook.' So, I cooked. Did I pass?"

The Chef's face was unreadable as a chopping block. "*You* said it was a test, Owen," he replied. "Not me. All I said was, I wanted to see what you could do."

Silence stretched out for a few moments as Owen thought back over their conversation the previous day. Was that true? Had Owen really gotten himself all worked up for nothing?

"But since you saw it that way," the Chef added, "let me ask you: Did you pass?"

Owen's shoulders slumped. "I don't know. I don't think so."

The Chef nodded. "Good. That's good, Owen.

"Let me tell you a secret. What inspires me most, every day, isn't what I already know how to do. A lot of people settle for that. But you can't become your best that way. Being impressed with what you already know won't get you to greatness. Not even in the ballpark.

"What inspires me most is what I *don't* know. What I can't do yet. There's not a lot of juice in being good. You know where there's a lot of juice? Finding ways to get better."

He paused, then added, "Tell you what else. If you'd said you thought you passed? That would've meant you flunked."

Owen started to laugh—but stopped abruptly when he realized the Chef didn't look like he'd meant that as a joke. "Wait. *Seriously?* But . . . you said it *wasn't* a test!"

"No," said the Chef. "What I said was, I never *said* it was a test. But then, I never said it wasn't, either."

Owen didn't know whether to feel offended or amused. His confusion made him feel embarrassed, and the embarrassment made him feel mad. Which made him think back on his angry breakfast—and that made him only more embarrassed, which made him feel madder . . .

And then, to Owen's great surprise, the Chef reached over and put a hand on his shoulder. And to his even greater surprise, he didn't pull away. Somehow, the weight of the Chef's hand felt solid and reassuring.

The Chef gave the boy's shoulder one brief squeeze, and then he stepped away toward the swinging doors again.

"You got a lot going on in there, Owen," he said over his shoulder. "A lot for a kid to carry. I'd say you're doing fine."

Owen lay on his bed that night staring at the ceiling, thinking back to another Saturday, years ago. *That's a lot for a kid to carry.* Those had been his father's exact words.

It had been early in the morning, not a sound in the house, when Owen slipped out of his bed and crept downstairs, still in his

PJs. Nobody could be up *this* early. But sure enough, when Owen reached the kitchen, there he was, standing at the island, apron on, his big hands resting on the island counter as he surveyed the display of ingredients and utensils.

"Hey, buddy," Owen's father said in a conspiratorial whisper, and he patted the empty stool next to him. Owen trotted over and wriggled up onto the stool to watch.

It was time to make The Recipe.

This was their Saturday morning routine; they'd been doing it for years, but it was still always exciting. They would make Owen's father's Famous Oat Blueberry Pancakes (Owen didn't know if they were *really* famous, but they were in this house, at least), and when they were finished, they would bring them upstairs on a tray, with hot coffee, to his parents' bedroom, where they would serve them to Mom in bed. Mom was always surprised when they walked in with the tray—and she always loved it.

As Owen grew older he eventually realized that she was only feigning the surprise. But there was nothing feigned about how much she loved the breakfast. Owen's father made the best pancakes in the world. Owen had always known this. But on this particular Saturday, sitting on his stool and watching The Recipe unfold, he had suddenly wondered why.

"What makes your pancakes so good?" he asked as his father dropped the batter onto the griddle in a series of calibrated spoonfuls. "Is it the oat flour?"

Owen knew they *always* used oat flour—not wheat, not pastry, not corn meal, not buckwheat, just 100 percent pure oat flour, milled fresh at the store.

His father smiled. He had the warmest smile of anyone Owen knew; whenever he smiled it made Owen's back feel warm, like the sun had just come out. "True," he said, "the oat flour does make them taste sweet and rich. . . ."

"And nutty?" Owen chimed in.

His father laughed. "And nutty. But that's not the secret."

"Is it the blueberries?" His father always brought home the most amazing, the sweetest, the juiciest blueberries from the farm stand near the high school where he coached. When blueberries were out of season, they might use cranberries instead, or sliced bananas, or even walnuts, and those were always good, but not *blueberry* good.

His father frowned and shook his head sternly. "*No.* That's *not* the secret."

Owen giggled. "Is it the honey? the oil? the maple syrup?"

"*No,*" his father frowned harder as he slid each finished pancake off the griddle onto a plate and dropped on more batter spoonfuls. "No, no, no!" Every time he said "no" it made Owen giggle more.

His father dropped the mock seriousness and let out that sunshine smile again, as he lifted Owen up off the stool with both hands and set him on the ground.

"The secret ingredient, Owen, isn't anything *in* the pancakes.

"The secret ingredient is who you're making them for.

"Now go get us a clean coffee cup, and we'll go serve the lady."

Now, lying on his back and staring at the bedroom ceiling, Owen tried to calculate how old he'd been that day. Seven? eight? He remembered wishing he was big enough to carry the tray upstairs himself and asking his father if he could try.

His father had looked at the tray: plate with stack of hot pancakes and sizzling sausages on the side; butter dish; hot maple syrup in gravy boat; napkin and silverware; coffee mug with thermal carafe. "Hmm." He looked over at Owen. "That's a lot for a kid to carry. Tell you what—"

He plucked a one-stem vase off the counter and handed it carefully to Owen with its lone occupant, a peach-colored rose.

"I'll carry the tray, you carry the flower. Deal?"

"Deal!" And Owen had led the way upstairs, tiny vase in hand with its single rose, as they did every Saturday.

3

the most important skill

When Owen arrived outside the diner the following week, he had mixed feelings.

The Chef had asked him to come in at "oh nine hundred" on Saturdays, their busiest day of the week. Owen's heart sank when he heard that. In his world, Saturdays were sacred. Not so much for blueberry pancakes (that ritual, like so much else in his life, had gone by the wayside since that day last September), but for *practice.* This new obligation put the kibosh on Saturday morning ice hockey practice, and the other guys had already given him a hard time about it, even his best friend Russ. He just hoped his Saturdays would free up again before baseball season started. Cutting out on hockey was bad enough. Missing baseball would be a disaster.

Still, as he parked and locked his bike he felt a shiver of anticipation.

He'd been practicing all week at home, flipping dried beans in a little skillet, and he was secretly looking forward to showing off his new skills with a perfect over easy egg. One morning that week his mom had even commented on how good the eggs were. Of course, that was Mom. She probably would have told him how good they were even if they were terrible.

If the *Chef* paid him a compliment, now, that would be something.

The next two hours were a blur.

The moment he walked in the front door Ruth called out "Morning, Handsome!" and immediately put him to work bussing tables. *Of course*, thought Owen. Why had he expected they would start him off doing any actual cooking? But he barely had time to register disappointment. The work flew at him too fast to think. The instant customers vacated a table he had to bring over a gray bus tub, place it on one of the chairs, clear all the dishes into the tub, wipe the table down, and then reset it for the next customer, all at lightning speed. And since there were more customers than seats, there was always someone waiting for a table to free up.

No wonder the Chef had asked him to come in on Saturday mornings.

When he wasn't bussing or taking out yet another bag in the constant parade of trash, Ruth had him mopping up the pools of dirty snowmelt being constantly trailed in through the front door. He had to follow a very specific and thorough sequence of steps every time he mopped. Apparently the Chef was a neat freak.

"Look sharp!" Ruth called as he headed for the swinging doors at the back with a full tub of dishes. "You don't want to get in Mad Dog's way."

Oh, great. The crazy breakfast cook was named *Mad Dog*? Owen would make sure to keep his distance.

By ten thirty things started slowing down. By eleven the place was quiet.

"Station!" the Chef called from the kitchen.

It took Owen a moment to remember what that meant. He was being summoned! He pushed through the swinging doors into the back and found the Chef standing by a small stretch of counter space at the far end of the kitchen, with a cutting board, a big chef's knife, a paring knife, a peeler, and a small stainless steel bucket half-full of water, with tongs and slotted spoons and various other tools sprouting from it.

As Owen approached, the Chef nodded at the cutting board. "Your station."

"Okay," said Owen.

"To work in this kitchen, you need to know five skills. Four I'll show you. The fifth, you'll tell me."

Another test, thought Owen. Was there always going to be another test?

The Chef held up his index finger. "First," he said, "you peel." He nodded at a fifty-pound bag of carrots next to where Owen stood.

It wasn't exactly making over easies, but at least it was dealing with food. Owen snatched up the peeler, pulled a carrot from the top of the bag, and set its tip on the counter.

"Hang on," said the Chef. He plucked a clean towel from a shelf and tucked one end into Owen's belt so that it hung down on his left side, exactly like the towel he always wore himself. "*Now* you're ready."

Owen took a deep breath. He knew it was silly, but he couldn't help it: like a superhero's cape or cowboy's bandana, having that towel slung at his side made him feel like a *chef*.

He set the carrot's tip on the board again and dragged the

peeler down the length of the carrot. One thin peel curled off. He turned the carrot slightly, then repeated the motion, taking care not to nick his fingers. (He knew first-hand how mean those peelers could be.) Then turned it again, and peeled again. And again. And again. When the carrot was finished he brushed his little pile of peels to the back of the counter, set the peeled carrot off to the side, and looked down at the bag.

One down. One billion to go.

He took another carrot and resumed peeling.

Ten minutes later, he stopped to assess his progress. He had peeled maybe twenty-five carrots. The bag looked almost as full now as it did when he started. He groaned. This would take all morning.

He looked up and realized the Chef was standing next to him.

"How's it going," said the Chef.

"Okay," said Owen unconvincingly. "Is there a faster way to do this? Like, a little dynamite? Maybe dunking them in a pool of piranhas?"

The Chef squinted briefly, as if the sun had suddenly gotten in his eyes.

Owen glanced around. There were no windows in the kitchen.

"As a matter of fact," said the Chef, "there is."

He took the peeler from Owen with one hand as he scooped up a fresh carrot with the other, then ran the peeler rapidly up and down the bottom half of the carrot, peeling in both directions as he rotated it. "Your peeler has two blades," he said as he went. "Might as well use both." A moment later he flipped the carrot over, now holding it by the tip, and shaved the other half. "See?" he said. The whole thing had taken seconds.

Owen saw, all right. He took back the peeler and started in on another carrot.

The Chef's trick worked like magic; twenty minutes later, he'd gone through the entire bag. He had to check his watch against the wall clock to make sure that was right. *Twenty minutes.*

A secret skill! He felt like James Bond.

The Chef was at his side again, scooping up all the peels and tossing them into a large tub at the back of the prep space.

"There's always an easier way to peel," said the Chef. "You can look at it as a chore, just hacking off peel after peel. Or you can look at this way: You're *opening up* the food. Getting to the heart of things."

He glanced at the boy to see if he was following this.

"When you meet a new friend for the first time," explained the Chef, "what do you do, first few times you're together?"

Owen thought for a moment. "I don't know. Talk, I guess? Get to know each other . . . find out if he likes baseball, or soccer, or whatever."

The Chef nodded. "Peeling."

He placed four or five carrots on the chopping block, then held up two fingers. *Skill number two.*

"Now, we cut."

Owen watched as the Chef went to work.

He sliced off the carrots' tips on both ends, then sliced them into several equal lengths. He cut one piece in half lengthwise, lay each half down flat and cut again, then tapped the four quarter-pieces into formation, butting their ends even with the flat of his knife. "Medium dice," he said, and he began chopping all four pieces at once, starting from the base, his left hand scuttling backwards like a crab being chased by the knife, producing what looked like a pile of little orange dice.

Only "chopping" seemed like the wrong word. Owen had expected the knife to go whacking rapidly at the board—*WHACK-WHACKWHACKWHACKWHACK!!*—but instead the Chef's movements were fluid and nearly soundless. It reminded Owen less of chopping firewood, which he'd grown up watching his father do every autumn, and more of times he'd watched his mom cutting out fabric to make him new clothes for the school year.

Snipsnipsnipsnipsnip . . .

The Chef was already on the second carrot, and now the third, pausing after each one just long enough to scoop up the little orange dice into a stainless steel bowl and then starting on the next, all in one continuous motion. It was almost weird: the Chef looked completely relaxed, like he had all the time in the world, and Owen could have sworn he was moving slowly—but that must have been some kind of optical illusion. Because that bowl was already *full*.

"Your turn," said the Chef. "Don't rush. Take your time." He handed Owen another chef's knife, much like his own, and said, "A chef's most important tool."

Owen was not looking forward to this. He'd made carrot sticks plenty of times at home and had more than one battle scar to prove it. He lined up a few carrots, the way he'd seen the Chef do, took the knife the Chef held out to him, and prepared to start cutting—

The Chef stopped him. "Like this," he said.

Owen looked at the Chef's knife hand, then at his own. He was gripping his knife the way he always did, his whole hand on the handle, like holding the handle of a suitcase. The Chef had *his* hand further forward on the knife, thumb and forefinger gripping the foot of the blade, and just his other three fingers wrapped around the handle.

"Choke up on the bat," murmured Owen. "Got it."

"*Choke up on the bat,*" the Chef repeated. His eyes did that strange squinting thing again, then he nodded. "Okay."

Owen placed his knife on his little carrot pile to slice off the tips—and was astonished at how easily the knife slid through. "Wow," he murmured.

The Chef nodded. "Your knives at home aren't that sharp."

"Not like this," said Owen, as he carefully cut the carrots into several lengths. "This thing is *scary*. Isn't it kind of dangerous to work with knives this sharp?"

"Other way around," said the Chef. "Dangerous *not* to."

This made no sense to Owen. "How can it be dangerous if they're less sharp?"

"It takes a lot of force to make a dull knife cut," said the Chef. "It's easier to lose control. A sharp knife takes less force, so it cuts where you want it to. Trying to become a great cook with a dull knife in your hand is like trying to play the piano with mittens on."

As the Chef spoke, Owen continued, cutting his carrot lengths into thinner strips, butting a group into formation, then chopping. But his pieces didn't look at all like the Chef's. The Chef's pile had looked like perfect orange sugar cubes. Owen's looked like a pile of rubble. Some pieces were larger, some much smaller, some of them cut in clumsy, irregular shapes. Whatever this was, Owen was pretty sure it wasn't a *medium dice*.

"This is pretty terrible, isn't it."

The Chef nodded. "Seen worse." He scooped up Owen's little rubble pile and tossed it into the same tub where he'd put the peels—*not* in the bowl where he'd placed his own pieces. "You can practice later on something softer, like zucchini." He nodded at the big pile of peeled carrots. "You're doing fine." And left him there to finish.

Owen lost track of time as he focused on his dicing. He wanted his carrot pieces to end up in the stainless steel bowl, not the reject pile. As he continued, the carrot pieces started looking a little less random, a little more uniform.

After a while the Chef appeared at his side, holding a spoon out toward him. "Taste?"

Owen hesitated. He had no idea what was in the spoon. "*Taste*," the Chef repeated.

He tasted. A flood of rich, warming flavors filled his mouth. "Delicious!" he said after swallowing his bite.

The Chef looked at him, eyebrows raised, like he was waiting for Owen to say more.

"Fish chowder?" said Owen.

The Chef looked at him without expression. "Yup. Fish chowder."

Somehow Owen felt like this had been yet another test—and that he'd just flunked. But what else was he supposed to say? He went back to his dicing.

Before long the Chef was there at his side again, another spoon outstretched. "Taste?"

Owen took this one right away. Rich and tangy: baked beans. "Mmm. *Really* good."

The Chef gave him that same inquiring look again.

Owen suddenly remembered his first visit to the diner, the week before, when they ate hot dogs together, the Chef saying, "Really good, *how?*" He closed his eyes. The beans were spicy on his tongue and made his mouth tingle. Owen groped for the right word. "Jazzy," he said.

The Chef squinted again. "Jazzy," he repeated, then said it once more: "*Jazzy*." He nodded. "Good, Owen. That's good." He held up the empty spoon toward Owen as if he were making a toast. "Baked beans Creole style. Sometimes we like to throw the residents of our town a little curve ball. Keep them on all their toes." He withdrew again, leaving Owen to his work.

By the time he had finished dicing all the carrots it was nearly noon, and he could hear the buzz out front, Ruth calling out dishes and slapping tickets up on the lintel of the pass-through (the "pass," as he'd learned it was called), the rhythmic clatter and hiss of Mad Dog working his Mad-Hatter magic on the grill. They were in full lunch crush now.

Owen looked around to see what he should do next.

"*Chef Special!*" he heard Ruth's voice call in through the pass.

Every day the diner featured a different Special, the Chef's take on a classic dish. Today the Chef Special was steak and onions.

Owen looked over at the Chef, who held up three fingers. *Third skill.*

"Now," said the Chef, "we cook."

He slapped a beef tenderloin down on the board, tossed a few three-finger pinches of salt and cracked pepper on it, then turned it and did the same on the other side, then shot a short squirt of olive oil into a cast iron skillet and dropped in the filet—*Tssss!*

As the filet sizzled he tossed in a few sprigs of some herb, then another, then smashed two cloves of garlic with the flat of his knife and tossed them in as well, followed with another dash of oil, then scooped up a pat of butter and tossed that in, too, then turned the filet over with a long set of tongs, a moment later turned it again—and then it was sitting on a clean plate as he spooned out the herbs and butter onto it.

"We'll let it rest while we make the sauce." They were the first words he spoke (and, with a single exception, the *only* words he spoke) as he cooked.

Into that same skillet he now added a dash more oil, then tossed in a small handful of what looked like chopped miniature onions—*Tsss!*—and gave the pan a shake, tossed in some salt and pepper, then tossed in a small handful of some strange-looking things Owen had never seen before that resembled floppy sea-shells, then flipped the skillet with another slight flick of the wrist (much as Owen had practiced with his dried beans), and all the little vegetable pieces lay down flat together like a pack of obedient puppies who'd been told, *Sit!* He then added in some other stuff from a row of small square stainless steel containers, a toss of this, a toss of that (Owen couldn't quite keep track of what they all were), then pulled the skillet off the fire and poured something from a bottle, put it back on the burner, ladled out some other liquid into it—

Then he dipped a spoon into the skillet, blew on it once, and held it out to Owen and spoke his one other word: "*Taste*"—

And Owen's mouth was suddenly alive with something peppery and salty and sweet and savory and indescribably amazing, something that tasted the way the Mapletown Fourth of July fireworks looked, dazzling against the inky summer sky.

Then those long tongs were snatching up the filet and now it was back in the pan, and then it was sitting on a fresh clean plate, the vegetable sauce spooned across it in a big swoosh.

Owen was speechless.

While the Chef handed the plate off to Ruth through the pass and Ruth said, "Another one, Chef," Owen stood rooted in place, staring at the stove, his mind on fire with everything he'd just witnessed, the skin on his arms tingling. For a moment, the boy forgot all about the ache in his chest, forgot about his unhappy life. His mind was filled with a single thought.

Someday, he told himself. *Someday I want to be able to do THAT.*

"Again," said the Chef, looking at Owen as if to say, *Watch closely now.*

He slapped another filet down on the board and reached for his salt and cracked pepper.

"Why salt and pepper it?" asked Owen. He was determined to catch every detail of the process this time around.

"You always season," the Chef said as he rubbed a few pinches into both sides of the filet. "The trick is not to overseason. You want your filet to taste like *itself*, not like salt and pepper."

"But if you want it to taste like itself, why do you add salt and pepper to it?"

The Chef replied as he added the beef to the hot skillet. *Tsssss!* "Most foods are very different on the inside than they are on the outside. Your goal as a chef is to draw out what's on the inside. To bring out its best."

Owen asked the Chef what the herbs were he was adding to the skillet.

"Rosemary," he replied. "And thyme."

"And what are those squat little oniony things?"

Owen had told himself not to be a pest and pepper the Chef with questions . . . but there was so much he didn't understand! As he watched the Chef walk through the dish a second time, the questions kept popping out, and the Chef calmly answered every one of them:

OWEN: What are those squat little oniony things?

CHEF: Cipollini. Like onions, only different.

OWEN: Different, how?

CHEF: Homework. Try some this week.

OWEN: And those little floppy seashell things?

CHEF: Wild oyster mushrooms.

OWEN: Why do you add butter when the steak is already nearly cooked?

CHEF: Absorbs all the flavors in the pan and pulls them together. You call that *deglazing*.

OWEN: Can't you get the sauce to be ready earlier, so the steak doesn't sit around cooling off?

CHEF: You *want* it to sit. It needs to rest for a few minutes, reestablish its equilibrium, reabsorb all its juices. Otherwise when you cut into it everything runs out and it'll be dry and tasteless.

OWEN: Why do you need a sauce anyway, if the steak is already perfectly cooked? Doesn't it just cover up the flavor?

CHEF: A good sauce adds moisture and brings out the flavor of the dish by complementing it, not overpowering it. Like a good wine complements the food.

OWEN: What are those? and those?

CHEF: Shallots. Green peppercorns. Here, taste—

Another spoon, and the fireworks again—

And the Chef's tongs shot out once more and the filet was on its plate, sauce swoosh and all, and in Ruth's hands.

Which was when the Chef turned to Owen and said, "Your turn."

Owen nearly fell over. He'd spent the morning bussing tables, mopping floors, and making a pile of rubble out of some carrots—and now he was supposed to cook the Chef Special? For a *customer*? What if he totally screwed it up?

"Jump in," said the Chef. "Water's fine."

Owen felt his heart hammering in his chest. He looked around frantically, trying to remember exactly which little square containers the Chef had taken his ingredients from.

"Take your time," said the Chef. "Don't rush."

Don't rush? thought Owen. Someone was out there waiting for his Chef Special—and he was supposed to *take his time*?

He slid a skillet onto a burner, shook in a few squirts of olive oil, and grabbed the filet the Chef had placed in front of him, about to toss it in the pan—when the Chef put a hand on his and stopped him.

"Owen," said the Chef. "Breathe. You have time."

Owen realized he'd been holding his breath. Looking into the Chef's eyes, he exhaled and took a deep breath.

"A lot of great cooking is patience," said the Chef. "Okay?" Owen nodded. "Okay. Now go ahead."

Owen salted and peppered his filet, then carefully placed it in the skillet—

"*Stop*," said the Chef.

Owen yanked the filet out again and froze, holding it in mid-air above the skillet.

"No sizzle," explained the Chef. "Pan's not hot enough. If you don't hear that sizzle when the meat hits the metal, stop what you're doing and get it out of there."

He looked at Owen and could see the *Why . . . ?* forming on his lips.

"You need it to get a good sear," he explained. "Locks in the juices. If you've ever had a dry, tough piece of meat, chances are good the cook did what you just did: put it in too soon. If the meat doesn't sear but just heats slowly as the pan heats, it'll suck out the moisture—and at that point it won't sear well no matter how high your flame. You end up with something like steamed meat.

"You might as well serve me boiled barn owl."

Owen glanced at the wall clock.

"Patience," said the Chef. They waited. After what seemed to Owen a geological epoch but was probably no more than five or six seconds, the Chef said, "Now try."

Owen touched the edge of the filet to the pan. *Tsssss!* The Chef nodded. Owen placed the filet flat in the pan, then looked around for the rosemary and thyme.

When the dish sat finished on its plate a few minutes later, Owen felt a flush of triumph. He'd made this! The Chef Special: courtesy of Owen Devon!

"Not bad," said the Chef.

Owen went over to the pass and peeked out at the diners. "Who's it for?" He turned back and saw the Chef holding the plate out to him. "You."

The Chef set the plate down toward the back of the prep counter, then held up four fingers. *Fourth skill.*

"But first, you clean."

The Chef pointed with his tongs to the six-inch-deep stretch of rail running along the front of the counter where Owen's cutting board sat. "Piano." Then he pointed his tongs at a damp rag sitting neatly folded at the end of the counter. "Rag." Finally he pointed the tongs at Owen. "The moment you finish, you wipe down your piano."

Owen grabbed the rag and swept it across the piano. The Chef took the rag from him and tossed it in a plastic pail of water—"sani bucket"—underneath the counter.

"Clean as you go, Owen. *Always* clean as you go. If you let it sit, food scraps and residue dry onto your piano. Or your knife, or your pan. And once something dries and hardens, it's a bitch to clean later."

"Okay," said Owen, but what he thought was *Really? That's a skill? Peeling, cutting, cooking—and* cleaning?

"This isn't like, 'Clean behind your ears,'" replied the Chef, as if Owen had spoken his thoughts out loud. "In a restaurant kitchen, cleaning is a matter of life and death. One out-of-control bacterial count can kill a customer."

"Seriously?" said Owen.

"Seriously. And killing customers is very bad for business."

Owen looked at him closely. Was he making a joke? It was impossible to tell.

"Okay, then," said the Chef. He nodded over toward the plated filet. "For you. Go ahead."

Owen pulled the plate over, took a fork and sharp knife, and took a bite. He closed his eyes. The filet was amazing—savory crustiness on the outside like a potato chip, tender as butter on the inside. It was the best steak he'd ever eaten, times a hundred.

"How is it?"

Owen opened his eyes. "*Phenomenal.*"

The Chef nodded. "And the sauce?"

Owen scooped up a bite of the vegetables. No fireworks. Just vegetables. "Pretty good," he said.

"*Pretty good,*" repeated the Chef, pronouncing the two words as if he were holding out a pair of smelly gym shoes with his fingertips. "Pretty good, *how?* Bland?"

"I guess," said Owen. "Yeah." Now that he thought about it, it *was* pretty bland. The filet was phenomenal . . . but the sauce was not.

"So here's the question," said the Chef. "While you were making it, did you taste it?"

Owen's face flushed. Thinking back, he realized that both times the Chef had made the dish, he had taken a fresh spoon and tasted the sauce, multiple times. When it was Owen's turn, he hadn't tasted his sauce once.

"I think . . . I think I forgot the green peppercorns."

The Chef nodded. "Garlic, too. And salt."

It was true! Rewinding back through the making of the dish, Owen realized that after first seasoning his raw filet, he'd never touched the salt again—and he'd completely forgotten about the garlic!

"Don't feel bad, Owen," said the Chef. "You did fine. You were copying what I did by watching me and thinking it through. But you can't cook by thinking. Being a great chef isn't about making up fancy dishes or being clever with a knife. It's about having a relationship with the food you're cooking.

"You can't make great food without *knowing* the food. And you can't know it with your head."

Owen took another bite of the vegetables and sauce. As he felt for the missing flavors, he thought back to the fish chowder the Chef had had him taste, and the baked beans Creole style, and that hot dog the first day they met.

Taste.

He looked up at the Chef.

"That's the fifth skill, isn't it. The one you said *I* had to tell *you.* Tasting?"

The Chef cocked his head and gave Owen a slow, appraising look.

Then nodded.

"That it is, Owen. That it is." He reached out and gave Owen's shoulder another brief squeeze, just as he had the week before, and once again Owen felt the weight of its wordless message.

Good job.

"Knowing how to peel, how to cut, how to cook, how to clean—they're all essential skills. But to be a great chef, Owen, none of those is number one. The most important skill?" The Chef tapped his forefinger to his tongue. "How to taste.

"*Taste everything.* That's Rule One."

Ruth caught up with Owen at the front door as he was putting on his coat.

"Bye-bye, Big Guy," she said. "See you next Saturday." She set her tray down and stood a little closer to him. "He likes you," she murmured.

Owen glanced back toward the kitchen to make sure they weren't being overheard, then looked up at Ruth. "I dunno. He seemed like . . . like I was bugging him."

Ruth frowned. "Bugging him, how?"

"I think I asked a lot of questions."

Ruth picked up her tray of dishes, turned, and headed back toward the kitchen, speaking over her shoulder as she went. "That's why he likes you."

☙

It was a fifteen-minute bike ride from the Mapletown Diner to Owen's home, and for all fifteen his head was buzzing with everything he'd learned that day, trying to keep all the pieces in order.

But it was the Chef himself he thought about most.

He was a hard guy to figure out. Did he ever smile? Or frown, for that matter? He didn't seem to have any expression at all, other than that weird squinting thing he kept doing. (And what was *that* about?)

And then there was how he had set Owen up to actually cook a Chef Special, like he was some kind of apprentice or chef-in-training. Which was crazy. He was only there to work off what he owed. Although that part, the part about feeling like a chef-in-training, that was actually okay with Owen. He would rather die than admit it to Russ or his other friends, but right now the idea of being a chef seemed pretty cool to him, maybe right up there with being a pro ball player.

By the time he skidded into his driveway he had made a promise to himself.

He was going to master that Special.

4

what a chef does

The moment Owen stepped inside the building the following Saturday he settled right into the routine, the bussing, trash-taking, and mopping already familiar to him. It felt strangely comfortable to slip into the flow and become part of this moving machine, to lose himself in the crazy pace of Mapletown Diner at peak operation.

What made it stranger (yet at the same time, somehow, more comfortable) was that he *remembered* this place. Or at least, he thought he did.

The flash came to him just as he finished mopping up a small mess of tracked-in snowmelt by the front door. Glancing up at the pastry case by the register, he had a dim memory of staring in through the glass front of that very display case at those donuts and Danishes, bear claws and bird's nests. Did they used to come here when he was little? He thought he remembered those counter stools, too, and running up and down the aisle, trying to get them all spinning at once . . . but when he tried to catch on to the memory, it slipped away like the melting snow.

"*Station!*"

By now the breakfast rush had slowed to a trickle, and the Chef was poking his head out through the pass.

Owen headed immediately back into the kitchen. "Carrots, Chef?" he said.

All that week he had practiced on zucchini (just as the Chef had suggested), and he was sure he could now do a much better job dicing those carrots. It wasn't easy finding zucchini in February in New England, and they weren't very good. He and his mom had eaten a *lot* of diced zucchini that week.

"We're good on carrots," said the Chef. "Today we need something else." There by his side at Owen's station stood a bag of onions.

Onions.

Owen hated chopping onions. They were hard to peel, awkward to cut, and they *always* made him cry. Owen hadn't cried in months, and he wasn't about to start now. No way.

"We'll dice them in a bit," said the Chef. "First, let's get them peeled."

The Chef picked up an onion and sliced off the pointy end, turned it over and set it down so that it sat on the flat cut he'd just made, then made one slice straight down through the middle, starting at the stubbly beard end, cutting the onion in two. He held up one half and pointed with his knife at the stubbly part. "Root," he said. "Leave that intact and it'll hold the whole thing together when you dice." He set his knife down and in one rapid motion unwrapped the half-onion, tossing the peel into the tub at the back of the counter.

"Your turn." He saw Owen hesitate. "Don't like working with onions?"

Owen shrugged. "Not so much."

The Chef looked at him close, then nodded slowly. "Tell you what. Let me show you the secret to cutting onions so they don't make you cry."

He took a fresh onion and once again trimmed off the stem end. "First, you have to use a sharp knife. When your cut is clean, you don't break open as many cell walls as you do with a dull knife. That's what releases that sulfur compound that gets to your eyes." He sliced this one in half, like the other, then pointed again at the stubbly root end. "If you cut the root, it starts bleeding juices—the sulfur stuff that makes you cry. So, leave the root."

He did that same one-motion unwrapping thing, then set the half-onion down flat. "Keep the cut side down on the counter till you're ready to dice. Less sulfur juice in the air." He peeled the other half and set it down likewise. "There you go."

"So," said Owen, "if you do all that, they won't make you cry?"

The Chef looked at Owen. "Nah. You'll still cry. Less, but still." He nodded at the onions. "Go ahead." As Owen gingerly trimmed off the stem end of his onion and sliced it in two, the Chef added, "You want to be a great chef, you cut onions. You cut onions, you cry. It's just how it is." He nodded at Owen's onion halves. "Good?"

Actually, Owen was surprised at how easily the peel came off when he followed the Chef's directions. It sure beat the way he'd always done it.

"Good," he said.

The Chef left him to his task.

While Owen prepped the bag of onions he kept thinking about what the Chef had said. *You cut onions, you cry, it's just how it is.* Something about that seemed so . . . unfair. He pushed his thoughts away and did his best to focus on slicing and peeling, slicing and peeling.

When the bag was empty, the Chef returned to his side again.

"Okay. Let's dice."

"Can I ask you something?" The Chef's eyebrows went up, and Owen figured that meant, *Sure, ask away.* "I know you said a chef's knife is his most important tool. I was just wondering, don't these knives look kind of . . . old?"

He was used to seeing chefs on TV with polished knives that shone like mirrors. Besides, any question that put off dicing those onions was a good question to ask.

"Carbon steel," replied the Chef, holding his knife blade up to the light. "Old school, but it holds a better edge than stainless steel—and it holds a better stain, too.

"As the blade stains, it starts telling the story of the chef who belongs to it. Every chef has his own set of knives, Owen. A good knife is like a good baseball glove. It only gets better with age. Becomes more *yours.*

"Okay? Let's dice."

He showed Owen how to hold his palm on top, with his fingers stretched out so they were out of the way, as he made several horizontal slices into the onion. He then made a series of vertical cuts through it—taking care not to sever the root—and finished the dice with another series of cuts at 90 degrees, moving from stem to root.

Owen tried one. It was amazing how much easier this was than when he'd cut up onions at home. And he had to admit: his eyes did not tear up that much.

While Owen worked, he thought about the knife he was using, and the stories its stain would tell if it could talk. *A good blade tells the story of the chef who belongs to it.* He wondered who belonged to the knife he was using now.

The Chef came back, holding out a spoon for Owen to taste.

Owen tasted it. "Fish chowder again," he said. The Chef said nothing, just raised his eyebrows again. *And . . . ?*

Owen was about to say, *What. It's the same chowder as last time*, when he remembered: he was supposed to really *taste* this. He ran his tongue along the inside of his mouth for a moment, then said, "It's different!"

"Different, how?"

"It's, I don't know . . . sweeter?" He took another taste. "But also . . . saltier?"

The Chef looked at him. "That's good, Owen."

Owen flushed with pride and embarrassment. The Chef didn't seem to notice. "This week," he said, "instead of potatoes we did half potatoes, half parsnips. That's the sweet. And we used a pancetta that's saltier than our usual bacon." He paused. "Good call," he added. Owen's cheeks went red again.

The Chef withdrew. Owen diced.

When he had nearly finished, the Chef returned and started scooping up the diced onions and putting them into containers as Owen polished off the last one.

"So how did it go, this week?" said the Chef. "With the Special?"

Owen didn't know how the Chef had guessed, but he was right. Zucchini was not the only thing he and his mom had eaten that week. In fact, Owen had spent every afternoon after school working to master the Chef Special.

And to be honest, it had not gone very well at all.

They couldn't afford filets, so he'd tried it with chicken breasts instead. Pretty dry. He also tried using a cheaper cut of steak once or twice. Kind of tough and not very tasty. But the big thing was the sauce. When they'd made the dish at the diner, all those vegetables were lined up in their little square stainless steel dishes ("squareheads," they were called), already peeled and prepped and ready to go. At home, Owen had to do it all from scratch. If peeling onions had seemed like a chore, peeling those little cipollini was murder. The shallots, too. And the garlic.

"Here," said the Chef. "Garlic is easy."

He grabbed a whole bulb of garlic, placed it upside down on the counter, and smashed it with the flat of his hand. All the cloves came apart. "Watch." He sliced off the root end of one clove and pressed it once with the flat of the blade, then gave it to Owen to peel.

To Owen's amazement, the garlic's papery husk came off easily.

"Shallots are a little trickier," said the Chef. He took a shallot, plucked a paring knife from the little water bucket on the counter (the Chef called it a "bain-marie") and made a single vertical slit along the shallot, then got his thumb under the skin and peeled the whole thing off in a single motion.

"Cipollini, they take a little patience." He took a cipollini, sliced off both stem end and root end, then with the paring knife began carefully pulling the skin down from the cut-off stem. In five or six peels, it was done.

"Wow." Owen had struggled like crazy with those little monsters, and the Chef made it look so easy. The Chef handed him a cipollini, and he did his best to reproduce what he'd just seen. As he worked, he tried to imagine peeling enough of these little things to make that filet dish just for two people, let alone for more. Was all this really necessary?

"So," he mused, "these are all basically onions, right?"

The Chef shrugged. "In a way. Same gene pool."

"So, would it work to just use onions, instead of the cipollini? And maybe chopped garlic, but skip the shallots?"

The Chef didn't answer Owen right away. He picked up the

vegetable pieces Owen had peeled and studied them, as if they held important information. "Tell me," he said, "have you thought at all about why you peeled those carrots last week?"

In fact, Owen had thought about that.

Taste everything, the Chef had said, *That's Rule One*, and Owen hadn't forgotten it. He'd peeled some carrots at home, and boiled them, and boiled some unpeeled, too, and tried his best to taste the difference. He even ate some raw carrot peels, to see if he could unwrap the answer that way.

"The peels taste sort of . . . I don't know, like paper?"

The Chef nodded. "And that's not necessarily a bad thing. The skin is rich in minerals and other nutrients. Sometimes you'll use the whole carrot, unpeeled, just as it is. For the dish I was making, I didn't want that.

"How do carrots taste? Sweet, yes, but it's a certain shade of sweet, with a bitterness in it, too, you think? Even without their skins, if you overcook them you can get that bitter taste. They're sweet—but not sweet like, say, maple syrup. Or yams."

"Or onions," Owen added.

"Or onions," the Chef agreed. "And onions aren't sweet like cipollini. Or shallots. Each one is different.

"To answer your question? Sure, onions would work fine. Steak and onions is a classic, and when you start with a classic, you can't go wrong. But a great chef doesn't stop there. You take a classic and then ask, *How can I improve on that?*

"A cook cooks. And there's nothing wrong with that, it's a noble thing. People need to eat. But a *chef* doesn't just cook. A chef transforms. A chef raises the level of everything he cooks. A steak. A sandwich. A hot dog. An egg over easy. A glass of water. You can improve *anything*. And you should seek to improve *everything*.

"That's what a chef does, Owen.

"*Improve every dish you touch.*

"That's Rule Two."

"*Special!*" came Ruth's call through the pass.

Owen had hoped for another crack at that filet—but no such luck. Today the Chef Special was . . .

"A salad?!" Owen had a hard time imagining salad being a meal. "That's the whole thing? Just a *salad*?"

"Not *just* a salad," said the Chef. "Watch."

The Chef tossed a pinch of salt and a squeeze of lemon juice into a pot of simmering water, then broke an egg into it (*an egg?!* thought Owen)—

Then grabbed a handful of delicate-looking green beans ("haricot verts," the Chef explained, "blanched"), sliced them in half and tossed them in a hot sauté pan, then tossed in a small handful of chopped shallots, followed by a few generous pinches of salt and cracked pepper—

Then he gently spooned some hot water over the poaching egg—

Then dropped some nuts onto the counter ("macadamias, toasted") and gave them a quick rough chop, scooped them up and tossed them in a stainless steel bowl on top of some frilly greens ("frisée") then followed them with a handful of croutons ("focaccia") and cheesy something ("bleu cheese crumbles")—

Then he placed a few pieces of cooked bacon on the board, gave them a rough chop, then pulled the green beans (no, *haricots verts*, Owen corrected himself) off the stove and tossed them on top of the greens, followed by the bacon—

Mixed some olive oil and vinegar from a tall, thin bottle ("*sherry* vinegar" emphasized the Chef, "sweeter") into a cup with a few smashed cloves of garlic and mixed it all into the bowl and poured its contents out into a beautiful serving dish—

Then scooped out the perfectly poached egg and gently placed it on top of everything.

"Chef Special!" he pronounced, and handed it off through the pass to Ruth.

Owen didn't ask why a poached egg, or why sherry vinegar, or why the macadamias and bleu cheese crumbles. He already knew. *Rule Two: Improve every dish you touch.*

"Another special, Chef!" said Ruth's disembodied voice—and Owen knew it was his moment in the sun.

"Your turn," said the Chef.

This time, Owen was ready. He had thought about this all week, and he was determined to do a perfect job. He stepped up to the stove—and froze.

He could not remember what came first.

"Salt and lemon," prompted the Chef.

Owen looked at him in confusion.

"In the water," added the Chef. "Keeps the egg together."

Oh, right! Owen grabbed a wedge of lemon, squeezed it into the water, and threw in a bunch of salt—too much, he realized, but it was too late to change that—then quickly cracked and added an egg.

Things had not gotten off to a good start.

He grabbed some haricots, chopped them in half, was about to toss them in a pan but caught himself just in time: he hadn't put a fire under the pan yet. He added a squirt of olive oil and heated the pan (*Patience, Owen*), then tossed in his haricots.

He turned to the grill and began spooning hot water over his egg to keep the top poaching.

"Pan," said the Chef softly. The haricots were starting to burn!

He yanked them off the burner, then added some minced shallots and let the pan cool for a moment while he chopped the macadamia nuts. Or tried to, anyway. But they acted like oiled marbles, slipping away from his knife every time he tried to cut them. It had looked easy when the Chef did it.

Breathe, Owen.

He took a breath and slowed down. They chopped just fine. He tossed them onto his bowl of greens, added the bleu cheese crumbles, then tossed it with dressing, put the haricots back on the burner—

He'd forgotten the bacon! He grabbed some cooked bacon, quickly rough-chopped it and added it to the bowl, tossed the salad a second time and dumped it out into a serving dish—

Then turned to fetch the egg out of its poaching liquid before it got too hard—

"Closer, bring your bowl closer . . ." murmured the Chef, but Owen was already in motion and not paying attention and pulled the egg from the water to carry it over to where the bowl sat waiting—

And dropped it.

Splat.

Owen stared at the floor in horror. There was poached egg everywhere. *Stupid, stupid, stupid!*

"Okay," said the Chef, as he moved the bowl toward the back of the counter. Owen didn't have to ask who this dish was for. Obviously this one wasn't being served to anyone. "You got flustered," the Chef added quietly as he stooped and cleaned up the egg. "It's okay."

Owen stood frozen in place, watching the Chef clean. Tears tried to sting his eyes but he wiped them away, furious and ashamed. *Improve every dish you touch*, he thought. *Yeah, right.* It seemed to Owen that he *wrecked* everything he touched. He felt like crawling into a hole and disappearing.

He felt the Chef's hand on his shoulder again. "It gets better, Owen," said the Chef. "It takes time, but it gets better."

When Owen got home, his mom was still at work.

Standing just inside the front door, he closed his eyes and tried to remember how the house sounded when they were all there together, the three of them. After a moment, he could hear it . . . the clatter of pans in the kitchen, scuffle of plates and dishes around the table, the talking and laughing all at once, the three overlapping each other. His father's voice booming in his ear, "GOOD JOB, buddy, GOOD JOB," his big hand on Owen's back.

What exactly had he done a *good job* of, that particular day, that had prompted his father to say that—something at school? at practice, or a game? Owen couldn't quite remember, and as he tried to pull the memory in tighter, it started slipping away instead.

In another moment it had all faded to nothing, and the house was silent again.

He let his breath out, opened his eyes, and stepped softly to the kitchen.

Usually when Mom had to work late he would put in something simple, like a whole baked chicken or a frozen lasagna. Tonight he wanted to surprise her. He'd stopped at the supermarket on the way home and gotten a little packet of bleu cheese. They didn't have sherry vinegar or macadamia nuts, but he figured their regular vinegar would do fine, and maybe he could use the almonds from their fridge.

This time, he did not drop the eggs. "*Good job, buddy,*" he whispered aloud, but that just made him feel lonelier.

A few minutes later his mom walked in. She looked beat, but her face lit up when she saw Owen, as it always did. She gave him a long hug, then pulled out a chair and sat down at the table. As she slowly, carefully pulled her shoes off her aching feet, she watched her son set down two big bowls of salad, a warm baguette in a basket in the center, a plate of butter, and a dish with some extra green beans.

"Wow," she said. "Fancy." She stood and planted a kiss on the top of Owen's head, hugged him again, then sat back down and put her napkin in her lap. She looked over at him. "You're an amazing kid, you know that, Owen?"

"Thanks, Mom," he said, then he added, "You're an amazing kid, too."

That comeback never failed to make her laugh, and it didn't fail him now. It made Owen feel good to hear her laugh again. Although it wasn't quite an all-out, all-there laugh, he noticed. More like the memory of a laugh. Still, that counted for something, right?

He told her about his day at the diner, about the Chef's methods for dicing onions and peeling garlic and cipollini, about all the ingredients in the Chef Special that day, and his Rule Two. His mom oohed and ahhed and groaned her way through every bite. Owen's monologue drifted to a stop, and they ate in silence for a few moments before he spoke up again.

"Mom?"

"What, honey?" she said as she reached to cut another slice of baguette. When Owen hesitated, she looked at him and put the bread down. "What is it, Owen?"

"Sometimes," Owen spoke quietly, barely above a whisper, "sometimes I try to picture his face, and I can't, exactly. I mean . . ." All at once his voice felt wobbly and hard to control, like riding his bike over a bed of loose gravel. "I mean, I have pictures in my room and everything. But sometimes when I close my eyes, it's like I can't remember exactly what he *looks* like. Like he's just – like he's just fading away."

Owen's mom stood up from the table and went over to him, wrapping her arms around him and talking softly into the top of his head. "*Never*. He'll never be gone, sweetheart. Never ever." She rested her cheek against his head for a moment, then spoke again. "It's okay if the pictures in your head aren't clear, honey, that's nothing to feel bad about. You're not a camera. You're a boy. You're his son. You'll *always* have him."

He didn't say anything, not because he couldn't think of anything to say but because he didn't trust his voice—and he definitely did *not* want to cry.

"I'm so proud of you, honey," she whispered.

He knew she meant it, too, though he couldn't see what he'd done that she would be proud of.

Lying awake in bed that night, Owen replayed the scene of that poached egg falling at the diner, the sense of hopelessness he'd had watching it ooze over the kitchen floor. For some reason it reminded him of school.

Maybe it was because his father had coached over at the high school that his own teachers seemed like they expected more of him than they did from the other kids. Whatever they expected, they weren't getting it, that was for sure. He'd overheard two of the coaches talking over his "case." He didn't hear much, beyond the doubt and disapproval in their hushed voices, but he did hear one hiss something about "headed for a bad future," and caught one word in the other's reply: ". . . appalling . . ."

Amazing, that's what his mom said he was. According to his coaches, the word was *appalling*. Owen didn't feel amazing right now, and he didn't think he felt appalling, either. He felt like he just wished things could be okay again, the way they used to be.

Improve every dish you touch, he thought. *It's what a chef does.*

He took a big breath and blew out the world's heaviest sigh. Staring at the ceiling, he thought about chopping onions in a way that they wouldn't make you cry.

After a while he fell asleep.

5

little things

On the third Saturday of his employment as a Mapletown Diner busser, gofer, and aspiring cook, Owen made a startling discovery. Mad Dog did not, in fact, bite.

It happened at a few minutes after nine. Having gotten a little careless in his routine, Owen charged through the swinging doors with his arms full of dishes and straight into Mad Dog's path, tripping over his foot and falling to the kitchen floor, dishes clattering everywhere.

I'm dead! he thought. Mortified at what he'd done, and terrified at what the lunatic breakfast cook's reaction might be, he looked up.

"Oh *maaaaaan*, are you *okay?*" Mad Dog was staring down at him, his jade green eyes wide with concern, offering him a hand up. Aside from the nearly constant mumbling to himself as he worked, these were the first words Owen had ever heard the cook speak.

"Thanks," said Owen as the cook helped him to his feet.

"No worries, man," said Mad Dog. And then he was back on his own planet, weaving and bobbing and muttering and clattering. "*Crème fraiche. Chilis. Chives, chives, cheddar, egg whites, egg whites only . . ."*

Owen dropped off his dirty dishes and went back out front to continue bussing.

About a half hour later, when he saw Ruth taking a short break as the pace slowed to a crawl, he went over to her.

"Hey, Ruth. Can I ask you a question?"

"Of course," she said.

Owen nodded toward the kitchen. "Why do you call him Mad Dog?"

She gave a faint smile. "It started as a joke, out of affection, but respect, too. He's the sweetest guy in the world. A ferocious breakfast cook, though. Get between him and his French toast and he'll run you down."

Owen was still trying to process the "sweetest guy in the world" part, but he got the "ferocious" part just fine. Mad Dog cooked like a forest fire, consuming everything in his path. He never paused, never stopped, never sat down to eat, and he would put down half a dozen cups of coffee by nine o'clock—Owen had seen him cook with his right hand while holding a coffee cup with his left. The only time Owen ever saw him come to a full stop was at about 10:30, when the mid-morning lull hit and the fresh roll delivery came in for lunch service. Then he would grab a roll, make a sandwich out of whatever was on hand, eat it standing up by the sink—and then rev back up into action again.

"I was here the day he interviewed for the job," said Ruth. "This was years ago. I greeted him at the door when he came in, and when he told me why he was here, I pointed him toward the kitchen. By the time he reached the swinging doors, Chef had made the decision to hire him."

"Whoa!" said Owen.

"Yeah," Ruth agreed, "and this after seeing five other applicants, all well qualified cooks, and turning them all down."

Ruth paused for a sip of hot coffee.

"One of our bussers at the time was a little sloppy (not like you, Owen). A party of three had just vacated a table, and a new party was taking their seats. The busser had quickly cleared the table but missed one dirty coffee cup. On his way to the kitchen Mad Dog stopped at the table, apologized to the customers, cleared the offending cup into a tub by the door, and slipped a clean cup onto the table.

"Chef saw him do it. That sealed it."

Owen tried to picture Mad Dog ambling toward the back of the diner, Mad Dog pausing thoughtfully, Mad Dog taking care of a customer's dirty coffee cup. "Wait, though. I mean, that's great, but what does that have to do with being the breakfast cook?"

"Let me put it this way," said Ruth. "How often do you hear people say, 'You *have* to try that place—their breakfasts are *amazing*'? Doesn't happen. But it does here. Most places, it's just eggs. Here, people come from four states just to eat our breakfasts. And there's one and only one reason for that."

Owen knew exactly what that reason was. "Rule Two, right? Improve every dish you touch?"

Ruth shook her head. "Mad Dog," she said. "Mad Dog's the reason.

"Have you noticed that the poached eggs here are always perfect—just soft enough so when you cut your fork into one the yolk runs out like slow-moving lava? That the over easies never have the slightest hint of crusty edge? That the scrambles come out exactly as the customer ordered, firm, soft, or medium?

"And here's a miracle for the modern age: the toast here is actually *hot* when it reaches the table! Where else on earth do you get hot toast? Who cares enough to time things so that the toast and eggs are hot at the same instant? Mad Dog.

"Mad Dog has a passion for great breakfasts. He cares enough to get every last detail just right. He seems kind of crazy, like he's a perfectionist—but that's not it. It's pure love.

"All those other applicants were competent cooks. But in that little, insignificant act, Mad Dog showed something better than competence. It showed that he *cared*."

Owen flashed on the Chef saying, *Most foods are different on the inside than they are on the outside.* Maybe that was true of most people, too.

Thinking of the Chef reminded Owen of something else he wanted to ask Ruth, and he could see her short break was at an end, so he blurted out, "Hey, can I ask you another question, quick?"

Ruth smiled and said, "I'd be disappointed if you didn't."

Owen leaned close and lowered his voice to a stage whisper. "Is there something wrong with Chef's eyes?"

Ruth looked puzzled. "His eyes?"

"Yeah," said Owen. "He keeps doing this squinting thing." He made his best effort to imitate it.

Ruth stifled a short laugh.

"What?" said Owen.

"Let me ask you something. Have you ever seen Chef laugh?"

Owen hadn't.

"Seen him smile, even?"

Owen shook his head.

"Well," she said, "that 'squinting thing' you're talking about? For Chef, that's rolling on the floor."

At that moment Owen heard the Chef's voice come flying out through the pass.

"*Station!*"

Owen was nervous about going back into the kitchen and seeing the Chef after making such a hash of his Special the week before, and even more so since his collision with Mad Dog this morning. But the Chef didn't bring any of that up.

This time the Chef had Owen peel and dice some onions—not a whole bag, just enough to fill a large bowl—and then peel and dice some carrots, which went into another, smaller bowl. Finally he pulled a few heads of celery from the walk-in. He showed Owen how to trim off the dirty root end and leafy tops, then wash and cut the ribs into manageable lengths, slit each piece lengthwise, and dice them to the same size as the carrots. The diced celery went into a third bowl, same size as the carrots.

As Owen diced, the Chef watched carefully. Every so often he pulled a piece out of the growing pile and tossed it into the same tub in back where he'd tossed the peels and other scrap bits. Some he rejected as too big, or too small. Some he deemed unworthy for reasons Owen didn't understand ("too odd") or seemed nonsensical ("too ugly").

When the dicing was finished, the Chef arranged the three bowls in a neat row on the counter and gestured grandly with both hands. *Ta-da*. "This, Owen, is mere—" and he said something that sounded to Owen like "pwah."

Owen looked at the bowls, then at the Chef. "Mere *what?*"

"*Mirepoix.* Humble beginnings. The dice that launched a thousand dishes. *Ten* thousand dishes. What you're looking at is one of a great chef's most important secrets."

Owen looked again. All he saw was onions, carrots, and celery.

"I know it doesn't look like much," said the Chef. "But the greatest accomplishments often don't, not at the start. Winston Churchill. Abe Lincoln. Rosa Parks." He grabbed a large cast iron fry pan and set it over a burner on a medium low flame.

"Rosa Parks?" Owen was feeling lost. What exactly were they talking about?

"So simple, but so powerful," the Chef was saying. "Mirepoix provides the foundation and flavor for more dishes than you could ever count. Soups, roasts, sauces, stocks, beans, stews . . ."

He squirted some olive oil into the pan, then added the onions, giving the pan a few good shakes so the pieces all got coated with the oil.

"To me, Owen, there's no more incredible aroma than sautéing mirepoix that has started to caramelize. Only in this case, we're not caramelizing it but *sweating* it—cooking over a low heat until they start to release their juices into the pan. Not searing to bring out their sugars, but slowly pulling out their inner taste. Very different from caramelizing."

As he spoke he added the carrots and celery to the pan, then shook the big pan a little so the new pieces all got exposed to the oil, too.

"Onions, carrots, celery . . . they're called *aromatics*, because they change the flavor and aroma of whatever you cook them with. Carrots have a kind of earthy sweetness, along with a little . . ." He looked at Owen, eyebrows up.

"Bitterness!" added Owen.

The Chef nodded. "The sweetness of a plant driving toward the earth's core. Then the onion's sweetness, which is sharper, more caustic on the outside, but more balancing and harmonizing on the inside. And celery has that wonderful salty grassiness, the taste of a plant reaching for the sky."

As the vegetables slowly changed, he added a little fresh chopped thyme and rosemary.

"They're all wonderful flavors—but they don't just add their flavors to other foods; they interact with those other foods. They *change* those foods. Sometimes, like with a roast, when the dish is finished you strain out the vegetable pieces themselves and discard them—"

"Wait," said Owen, "you throw them *out?*"

The Chef shrugged. "They've done their work. They've transformed the dish."

"Yeah, but . . . you throw them *out?* I don't get that," said Owen.

The Chef thought for a moment. "When you were little," he said, "did you have a favorite teacher?"

Owen didn't have to think to answer. A memory flooded in, unbidden—a face, and even more the warm velvet voice that went with it, the cozy feeling of that voice reading stories aloud, that thrill of excitement and adventure and security all wrapped together.

"Miss O'Malley," he said. "Second grade. She used to read us books."

The Chef nodded. "When was the last time you actually saw her?"

"Years, now. Five, six years?" Owen counted backward in his head. "No, seven!"

"But you're still a different person today for having known her," said the Chef. Now he added some crushed garlic to the pan. "That's what mirepoix does. It changes the other ingredients in that dish, and the dish will never be the same again."

He looked at Owen.

"You know what I'm saying, Owen? Miss O'Malley may be gone from your life—but she's not *gone* from your life. She changed you, and that change is still there. So *she's* still there. She always will be."

Thinking about Miss O'Malley and second grade brought

back a flood of memories, and with them a wash of feelings that were almost overwhelming. What had his mom said? *You'll* always *have him.*

With an effort, Owen pushed his feelings aside and his attention back to the present.

The Chef was emptying the pan's contents into a large pot. When he finished doing that, he disappeared into the walk-in and came out with a covered five-gallon bucket.

"Now, the secret ingredient. Liquid gold." He began pouring the bucket's contents into the pot, too.

"Liquid gold?" repeated Owen.

The Chef nodded. "Stock."

As Owen watched the golden liquid flood the pot, he thought about what the Chef had said about *aromatics.*

"If we're using them just for what they add to the other ingredients," he said, "why do we need to cut every piece exactly the same size? I mean, I get that it looks professional. But does it really make any difference to the dish itself?"

"It makes *all* the difference," the Chef replied. "The cut is critical. Mirepoix will act differently depending on how you cut it, and how you cut it depends on how you're going to use it. Cooking time determines the size of the pieces. Shorter the cooking time, smaller the cut, so the pieces release their flavor faster. For a roast, like prime rib, you'd cut your mirepoix in big chunks for long-time cooking. I'd probably have you leave the carrots unpeeled, too. But not for today."

Owen had been determined to figure this out himself, but he couldn't hold back the question any longer: "So what exactly *is* it that we're making?"

The Chef called out over his shoulder as he headed back into the walk-in again. "The Original Medicine, Owen. Elixir of Life.

Grandma's Apothecary." He emerged with a covered tub and plopped it on the counter. "Jewish Penicillin."

Owen looked at him, his face a blank.

"Chicken soup, Owen," said the Chef.

"Oh," said Owen.

The Chef took pieces of poached chicken from the tub.

"Here's the rule of thumb when you're making mirepoix for a soup: it needs to fit on the spoon. Your customer needs to be able to eat it without having to cut it, and without choking on it. Your pieces need to be big enough so they don't fall apart, small enough so they don't stand out."

He began dicing the chicken to the same size as the mirepoix he and Owen had made.

"The secrets to a beautiful soup: everything is cut perfectly, to uniform size and shape; the broth is totally clear, with no fat floating on top; and the chicken is done perfectly. It's incredibly simple, but it takes a lot of care—in the cutting and especially in the timing. That's the chef's responsibility.

"If you don't pay attention, you get mushy carrots, tough or shredded bits of chicken, broth that's cloudy and confused—a soupy mess where you can't quite taste anything, because nothing is clear.

"Sometimes a chef overthinks or complicates. Sometimes the simplest things are the most beautiful. Sometimes our responsibility as a chef is just not to mess up what's there. Pay attention to the details. How you cut your carrots. How you clean your knife. How you sweat your onions.

"The Buddhists have an expression, Owen. *How you do anything is how you do everything.*"

Owen thought about what Ruth had said, about Mad Dog clearing away a single used coffee cup and the Chef watching him do it, and something he'd heard in school came back to him. "Our English teacher says, the devil is in the details."

"Is that right," said the Chef. "Myself, I'm partial to how that great architect Mies van der Rohe said it. *God is in the details.* In any case, God or the devil, I can promise you this: *greatness* is in the details.

"And that's Rule Three, Owen. *Pay attention to the little things.* When you do, the big things tend to take care of themselves."

Ruth's voice came through the pass:

"*Special!*"

Owen hadn't seen the menu today and couldn't wait to find out what today's Special was. After a filet with peppercorns and wild mushrooms, and a frisée salad with sherry vinegar and macadamia nuts and a poached egg, how did you top two classy dishes like that?

"*Grilled cheese sandwich?*"

Owen figured he had eaten probably a thousand grilled cheese sandwiches in his lifetime. Two slices of white bread, two slices of American, and butter in a pan. How did *that* rate being a Chef Special?

"Rule Two, Owen," was all the Chef would say. *Wait—which one was that again?* Owen was about to ask—but the Chef was already at work. He pulled something from the cooler ("fresh jumbo lump crab") and mixed it with a few pinches of salt and cracked pepper in a small bowl, then added a few shakes of cayenne and a squeeze of fresh lemon—

Then grabbed a few sprigs of fresh dill, minced about a teaspoon's worth, and added that to the crab mix, followed by two dollops of mayonnaise—

Then spread the resulting mixture over a piece of thick, dense bread ("brioche: eggy, nice")—

Then grabbed a cucumber, ran the peeler along its length in long strips, alternating peeled and unpeeled sections so that the cuke looked like it was painted with green and white stripes, then rapidly knocked off a half dozen thin slices and layered those on top of the crab mix—

Then pulled out a block of creamy whitish cheese ("brie—something different") and added slices of that on top of the cukes, followed by very thin slices of what looked like a black mushroom ("truffle—" the Chef paused for one split second and held up one forefinger as he added: "the bomb") and topped it all with a second slice of the brioche bread, buttered it on top, flipped the whole thing with a spatula onto the surface of the hot steel griddle and buttered the now-exposed other side.

"While this cooks," he said, "let's finish the soup."

He took a bunch of—parsley? no, *cilantro*—and chopped it fine, his knife a blur (*like the needle on Mom's sewing machine*, Owen thought), talking as he went.

"Parsley would work, too, or dill, but cilantro is an interesting twist that tugs it gently in a different direction, but doesn't violate the basic idea of chicken soup. You could add more heat, like chilies and lemongrass, and take it in a Thai direction, or leave it simple and add some nice dumplings and make it heartier. Today, we'll go this way."

He ladled out some soup into a bowl, tossed in some cilantro, and then squeezed a wedge of lime over it.

"The heat of the soup is going to release most of the flavor and perfume from those delicate greens, so you want to do it right before serving. Your thyme and rosemary, they're heartier herbs, they can go in at the beginning when you're sautéing, but the finishing herbs, the *fines herbes*," (he pronounced it *feen-zairb*) "they want to go in right at the end."

He dipped in a clean tablespoon, lifted it to his lips, and closed his eyes. "Ahhhh." He opened his eyes and looked at Owen. "*This* will heal anything you can throw at it."

Turning back to the griddle, he flipped the sandwich over with his spatula, then picked up his chef's knife again and pointed with it at the tureen of soup.

"The cilantro will stay that fresh, beautiful color for ten, maybe fifteen minutes, tops, before it degrades into a full army green. Which is, I'm sorry to say, not beautiful at all."

He turned back to the sandwich again.

"Now if you want to go fancy, you can trim off the crusts and cut the trimmed sandwich into small bites. For today . . ."

He cut the sandwich in half on the diagonal, laid one half down on a plate and then placed the other, tipping and leaning it onto the first, then handed the plate off to Ruth's outstretched hand, announcing it as he did:

"Chef Special: soup and sandwich."

Owen knew what was coming next.

"Okay? Your turn."

Owen had watched the Chef's every move as closely as he could. He was starting to get the hang of how to observe the Chef in operation and catalogue the steps in his brain. Even with the fancy additions (the crab and brie and cayenne and all), this dish honestly didn't seem too complicated. Plus, the soup was already finished, aside from adding a little chopped cilantro and a squeeze of lime to the bowl.

For probably the first time since that morning three weeks

earlier when he'd been so cocky about his over easy eggs, Owen stepped up to the grill feeling somewhat confident. He took a breath, took his time, took in all his ingredients in a glance—and reached for the crab.

To his relief, not only did he make no major mistakes, but the thing actually came out pretty well.

Mad Dog swooped in, one hand out, and slapped Owen a high five. "That's what I'm talkin' about!" he grinned. The Chef said not a word, but Owen knew his face well enough by now to see that, even though he showed practically no outward sign of it, he was pleased with Owen's effort.

"Who are we serving it to?" Owen asked, knowing that the Chef would reply, *You.*

The Chef slid the plate over closer to himself and said, "Me."

Seeing the look of surprise on Owen's face, the Chef squinted briefly. (*Rolling on the floor*, thought Owen.) "*And* you," he added, taking one half-sandwich off the plate for himself and then pushing the half-empty plate back toward Owen. "Let's eat. We earned it."

Owen took a bite.

It was like ice cream, Christmas, his mom's best medium-rare cheeseburgers, and heaven, all exploding in his mouth at once. *How did grilled cheese rate being a Chef Special*, he'd wondered. He had his answer. And now he remembered which one was Rule Two:

Improve every dish you touch.

As they ate, Owen thought back over the process of cooking the sandwich. Something was bugging him. "I do have a question," he said.

The Chef raised his eyebrows. *Yes?*

"It seems like every time I use the salt, or the pepper, or the butter, or . . . well, just about anything, after I put it back again, you move it."

The Chef thoughtfully chewed his bite of crab and brie.

"I mean," Owen went on, "I get that it's important to keep everything neat. Like, greatness in the details and everything. But why does it matter if the olive oil is on the left, or on the right?"

The Chef looked at Owen, then took another bite, chewed, swallowed.

"If I told you I was going to cater a luncheon for upper-crust CEOs in New York City tomorrow, and I was going to serve them grilled cheese, you'd say I was crazy." (Was the Chef completely ignoring his question? Had he even heard it?) "But I could serve them this, and it would be the talk of the boardroom."

The Chef brushed his hands off on each other, signifying that he had finished chewing and savoring every morsel, then nodded, as if he had made an important decision, and looked directly at Owen.

"Next week, can you come in early?"

"Sure," Owen replied. He thought for a moment, then said, "Wait—how early is early?"

"Oh five hundred," said the Chef. "On the dot."

That night Owen took out a sheet of notebook paper and wrote down the Chef's three rules, to help him remember which was which.

Rule 1: Taste everything.

Rule 2: Improve every dish you touch.

Rule 3: Pay attention to the little things.

". . . And the big things tend to take care of themselves," he murmured.

He lay on his bed and stared up at the ceiling. Part of him was afraid that was not true at all. Another part of him hoped that it was.

6

the batter's box

On the dot of five the following Saturday morning, when Owen pulled up to the diner on his bike, the Chef was standing out front, his breath billowing overhead like great steam clouds. He nodded at Owen and unlocked the door. It was a bitter March day, cold as the diner's walk-in freezer. Owen's face was numb.

"What do you w-want me to do, Chef?" said Owen as he followed the Chef inside.

"Watch." The Chef stamped the snow off his feet as his hand went automatically to the light switch and flipped it on.

"Okay," said Owen, stamping off his feet likewise. "Watch, and do what?"

"Just watch." The Chef strode straight back toward the kitchen, Owen at his heels. Pushing through the swinging doors, he flicked on the coffeemaker, which was already loaded and ready to go (the Chef was not a coffee drinker, but the others certainly were), then turned on the ovens and griddle. Owen longed to stand right by the ovens (he couldn't feel his fingers—how long would it take for the place to warm up?), but he dutifully followed as the Chef headed into the walk-in and wheeled out a tall metal rack with twenty-five or thirty sheet pans in it. Owen got a glimpse of what was in there: flats of raw bacon, already portioned and ready to go.

The Chef positioned the rack by the oven, then returned to the walk-in and came back out wheeling a second rack, this one with roasting pans of sausage and breakfast potatoes, cut and mixed with chopped onions and green peppers and ready to cook. (*They must do all that prep in the afternoon*, thought Owen, though he so far had never stayed through the afternoon to see it.) The Chef brought his second rack to a stop next to the first, then walked over to the pot sink, grabbed a little stainless steel bain-marie and filled it halfway with water, grabbed his tools—spatulas, tongs, metal spoons—and dropped them in, then collected his pots and sauté pans and arrayed them all out on the counter by the pass, then turned on the burner under a small kettle of water—

And took a breath.

As the ovens warmed, he stepped into his office back in a far corner of the kitchen, behind the storeroom. Owen followed. The Chef took off his coat, put on an apron, then came back out into the kitchen where the kettle was now whistling: time for tea.

It was 5:20.

After taking a few sips of his hot tea, the Chef slid the trays of bacon and sausage into the ovens. He emptied two racks of the potatoes, onions, and peppers onto the now-hot griddle. They hit the gleaming steel surface with a loud *Tssssss!* and settled into a medium sizzle, skittering gently in bacon fat as they slowly began caramelizing to a beautiful golden brown.

"Nothing like the smell of fresh bacon and onions in the morning," the Chef commented as he glanced around the kitchen, king of his domain.

"Now, the eggs."

Owen watched the Chef pull out a case of eggs from the walk-in and empty it, flat by flat. Owen counted ten flats, thirty eggs to a flat . . . that was *three hundred eggs*.

The Chef flattened the empty box and tossed it in back, then placed a three-gallon bucket on the counter with a big conical strainer over it ("China cap"), and then two smaller tin cans next to the bucket, one on each side. Next he placed five flats of eggs off to the side of one can, another five next to the other. Picking up an egg from each side, right and left hands working at the same time, he cracked both eggs one-handed, each on the lip of its respective tin can, then dropped their contents into the strainer and the empty shells in the two cans, talking as he went.

"These are for scrambled and omelets," the Chef explained. "The rest, like over easies and poached, we do to order."

He kept repeating the sequence, like a machine, until the flats were empty. Owen timed it. *Seven minutes to crack the case*, he thought. *Better than Sherlock Holmes.*

It was 5:45.

The Chef opened the oven, grabbed the hot sheet pan of bacon with his side towel in one hand and tongs in the other, placed it up on the counter, where he removed all the bacon to a resting rack with his tongs, then used the tongs again to scrape the baking paper into the trash, all in one unbroken movement, like a pro hockey skater stealing the puck and swooping around to land a goal.

He grabbed a roasting fork and wedged it into the handle of the hot pan, lifting and moving it effortlessly to the back. It was as if the roasting fork was an extension of his hand, a living part of him.

"There's nothing like the sense of satisfaction of having your station set up perfectly and ready for war," he said. "Every spoon, spatula, sauté pan, everything exactly where it needs to be—completely clean, uncluttered and ready. No sight more beautiful."

It was 5:55.

Owen heard the front door of the diner unlocking, opening, then locking again. "Morning!" came Ruth's voice drifting back through the pass. She would unlock again in five minutes for their first customers of the day.

The Chef poured himself a fresh cup of tea.

For the next three hours straight the Chef cooked, and Owen watched, transfixed.

He had thought it would be boring to do absolutely nothing but stand there and watch someone cook breakfast after breakfast after breakfast. He was wrong. It was riveting.

At first he could hardly process what he was seeing. Only it was more what he *wasn't* seeing. Owen had seen Mad Dog cook, and that was like watching a tornado on the Weather Channel: hands flying everywhere, clattering and rattling and banging, and the near-constant drone of the cook's running muttered monologue. He'd also watched chefs on TV running around their studio kitchens, racing from shelf to stovetop to chopping block, flipping things in the air as they ran in a dazzling display, like Cirque de Soleil, but with food.

The Chef was nothing like that.

If anything, the opposite. It seemed to Owen as if he hardly moved at all, his body rooted to the floor, face impassive as a statue, so much so that Owen actually wondered once or twice if he might be napping while standing there.

He obviously wasn't napping, though—because dish after dish

flew out of his tiny station. When Owen glanced at his watch to see if an hour had gone by yet, he was startled to find that it was nearly nine. He figured a good hundred breakfasts had to have come out of the Chef's station while he'd been sitting there watching. That was more than one new breakfast every two minutes—for three solid hours!

The whole time, he hadn't seen the man take a single step.

At nine o'clock Mad Dog showed up (he'd been given the early morning off) and the Chef finally took a break. He brewed himself a third cup of hot tea, then took Owen out back onto the little loading dock behind their building where they took deliveries. The two sat on the dock, their legs dangling off.

The Chef took a sip of his tea, then another. Finally he said, "So what did you learn?"

"How do you *do* all that?!" Owen didn't mean to answer a question with a question, but his curiosity had been at a high simmer for the past few hours. "It seemed like you hardly moved. When I make breakfast at home, I run back and forth around our kitchen at least five or six times—and I'm only cooking for two!"

The Chef replied with a single word, but Owen didn't catch what it was. It sounded like he said *meezonblahs.*

"Sneezing blahs? Methuselah? Beelzebub?"

"*Mees*-ohn-*plahss,*" said the Chef. "It's spelled M-I-S-E, E-N, P-L-A-C-E. That's French for *put in place.* Meaning, you put everything you need to cook where you need it—your salt and pepper, your knives, your whisk, your tongs, your oil, your butter—get it all arranged so it's within easy reach and you always know exactly where each item is. You want to be able to operate within a three-foot square, and not have to run off to the cooler while you're in the middle of a dish and throw the whole production off."

He looked at Owen. "You see?"

"Like a batter's box," said Owen.

The Chef frowned, then slowly nodded. "Okay. Yeah." He seemed to consider that for another moment, then nodded again. "Your batter's box. You don't swing until you know exactly where you're standing. That's good.

"*Mise en place* means your space is clean, organized, clear of clutter. Which allows your mind to be uncluttered. When you clear your space, you clear your mind. So you can focus one hundred percent on what you need to focus on, and nothing else—no distractions, no nonessential tasks, no unnecessary movement.

"To a chef, *mise en place* is more than a technique or a strategy. It's practically a religion. Which is why a chef can't stand it when someone else moves their stuff."

"Okay," said Owen. "But . . ."

The Chef raised his eyebrows. *But?*

Owen was still thinking about how the Chef would move something after Owen had put it back, sometimes even just a few inches.

"It seems kind of . . . extreme."

The Chef drained his cup, then got to his feet. "Tell you what," he said, as Owen followed him back into the kitchen. "Grab a menu—" he snatched a menu from a shelf as they stepped over to the stove and handed it to Owen "—and pick any item. Whatever you want. I'll make it for you."

Owen scanned down the list. Ever since his first visit, he'd wanted to see the Chef cook an omelet again. "Omelet," he said.

"Okay," said the Chef. He pulled a bandana from his back pocket, reached up, and tied it around his head, knotting it in back. A blindfold.

Wait. A *blindfold?*

"There are two secrets to a good omelet," said the Chef. "The first is, use *really* fresh eggs. It makes a difference." He picked up an egg and cracked it into a bowl, then another, then a third.

Owen's mouth hung open. How was he *doing* that? How did he even know exactly where the eggs were, let alone exactly where the lip of the bowl was?

"But the real secret," the Chef continued, "is to use medium heat. Patience!"

He grabbed a whisk from the bain-marie and briskly whipped the eggs into a light froth.

"Most times you get an omelet, it has that bit of brown crust. If you watch what you're doing, you won't get that. A classic omelet is the same lovely cooked-egg color throughout."

He scooped up a generous pat of butter and dropped it in the pan, where it immediately began melting.

"Some people add a little cream or milk to make it richer and fluffier. I use just a dash of water."

He plucked a wooden spoon from the back of the counter, then poured the egg mixture into the pan.

"You don't scramble it, exactly, you sort of semi-scramble, *encouraging* it, so you always have fresh raw egg mix moving to the pan's surface."

Owen watched as the Chef gently pulled the egg mixture from the edge toward the center, continuing around the pan. As he herded the egg toward the center, fresh raw egg ran around the sides of the spoon and out to the edge. Now and then, as more egg collected in the center, he smoothed it back out to the edges with the spoon, as if he were icing a cake. Meanwhile he rotated the pan gently with his left hand, in light circular movements back and forth, so the whole thing was a two-handed dance.

"You semi-scramble like this for twenty, thirty seconds, till you've got it all circulated and starting to set—not raw, but still soft on top. The inside should be soft and silky."

He set the pan down for a moment.

"Some people flip the omelet," the Chef continued. "I'm not a fan. I don't like it to dry out, I want it to stay moist."

Meanwhile he reached out with his right hand, grabbed a slotted spoon, and spooned a small amount of what looked like sautéed onions from a pan on a back burner, then spooned it out in a line along the middle of the omelet as he talked.

"Your garnish should be precooked or sautéed in another pan—your spinach, mushrooms, onions, ham, whatever. For you: my special New England omelet."

He then reached out, again with his right hand, and scooped up some bright yellow grated cheese from one of those square-heads and scattered it on top of the onion mix.

"Slices of tart apple from New Hampshire, cooked with sweet onion from Massachusetts—plus grated cheddar from Vermont."

Owen was wide-eyed. How was the Chef seeing where to grab all these ingredients from?

"There are two ways to go, now. You can do a French roll, folding it in from both sides, or—" and he demonstrated this as he described it "—half-moon style" and he slid the finished omelet onto an empty plate that somehow happened to be sitting in just the right spot, and with the pan itself gently folded one half of the omelet over the other.

He put the empty sauté pan back down on the griddle, reached over with his left hand and plucked up a fingerful of chopped scallions, dropping them artfully on top of the omelet.

"The trick," he said as he untied his blindfold and stuffed it back in his hip pocket, "is to carefully work the pan, making sure you don't get any browning to it. And keep your flame at medium height. A lot of great cooking is patience. As I mentioned before."

Owen stared at him.

"Of course," the Chef added, "if you're in a production line and have to crank out dozens of omelets fast, there are some tricks. You put each person's garnish in its own coffee cup as you go, so you know who gets what. And you might throw a half-done omelet under a broiler or salamander to set the top. I might even flip them in the pan, if things are busy enough."

"How . . ." Owen began, but his throat was too dry to talk. He cleared his throat, coughed, and tried again. "How did you . . . ?"

Where should he start?

The Chef waited.

Owen thought about it all for a moment. *Why does it matter if the olive oil is on the left, or on the right?* he had asked the week before. He remembered wondering whether the Chef had even heard the question. But he'd heard, all right, and Owen had just gotten his answer.

The Chef knew his batter's box.

"Wow," was all Owen could think of to say. He was still replaying the scene, the Chef standing there rambling on as he cooked a perfect omelet—*blindfolded.*

"You can start," said the Chef, "by picking a single dish and making a complete list of everything you need. Write it down. Gather everything on the list. Then cook—and you'll see if you left anything out. If you did, add it to the list. Perfect the list. Memorize it. Then throw it away. Because now it's part of you."

"You learned all that *mise en place* stuff in culinary school?" said Owen.

"Actually, I learned it in the army. They just didn't call it that."

"What did they call it?" asked Owen.

The Chef shrugged. "They called it, *being in the army*."

Owen thought for a moment. "But . . . how did you know when the omelet was done? It's not like you could see it. How did you know there wasn't still a bunch of raw egg in there?"

"First, I could feel the consistency of the egg. Through the wooden spoon. And besides," he tapped one finger to the side of his nose, "you can smell when it's done. Remember Rule One, Owen: *Taste everything*—and not just with your tongue. You cook with *all* your senses."

Owen spent the next hour bussing late breakfast dishes and helping out with a few prep tasks for lunch. But he moved automatically, as if in a dream, his mind still replaying that blindfolded omelet sequence.

When it was nearly time for him to leave, the Chef asked if he could see him for a moment, back in the office.

"Yes, Chef?" said Owen, poking his head in the office door.

"Come in for a sec, Owen."

Owen stepped into the tiny office and sat in the little folding chair by the door.

"How are things going, Owen? At school?"

This was not a conversation Owen wanted to have. Things at school were terrible. His Saturdays at the diner had started to feel like little oases in his life—but the rest of the week was still one long stretch of desert. "Okay, I guess," he said.

A few moments ticked by.

"*Mise en place* isn't just about being neat and organized in the kitchen," said the Chef.

"Okay," said Owen.

The Chef thought for a moment, then said, "If you want to get somewhere, you put your effort into controlling the sail, not the wind. You understand what I mean by that?"

Owen wasn't sure if he did or not.

"You can't determine what happens, Owen. You can't control the universe. But you can direct your own thoughts and actions. You can compose the space directly around you. That's what *mise en place* is about."

When he didn't say anything else, Owen said, "Is that another rule?"

The Chef nodded. "That it is, Owen. Rule Four: *Compose your space*."

Owen thought about that as he got his coat, unlocked his bike, and pedaled for home.

Put your effort into controlling the sail, not the wind.

He thought about his friends, and school, and his teachers and coaches. He thought about his mom, and the ache in her eyes, and how much he wished he could protect her and make her sadness go away. He thought about how much time he spent in his bedroom, staring at the ceiling and wishing his father was still here.

It didn't feel to Owen like much of anything in his life was under control right now.

So what exactly was the wind, and what were the sails?

7

spring

As the weeks slipped by, Owen continued peeling and dicing, learning the tasks of basic prep and care of the kitchen, helping with breakfast and lunch, and learning each new Saturday's Chef Special.

He also learned all sorts of variations on the mirepoix theme. For fish chowder, to keep the stock a lighter color, they used leeks in place of carrots. Sometimes the Chef added diced mushrooms, parsnips, or shallots, or even diced ham or pork belly. One Saturday the Chef made a Creole dish with a mirepoix of onions, green peppers, and celery. "Cajun cooks call this the Holy Trinity," said the Chef, which Owen found hilarious.

Then there were all the regular dishes, too. Owen started paying more attention to what was happening over on Mad Dog's side of the kitchen, and got to observe the fine points of dozens of dishes—variations on tuna salad and chicken salad, grilled cheese and BLTs, burgers and Reubens, chowders and stews, and of course, eggs and eggs and more eggs. At night he dreamed of omelets and thin-sliced tomatoes and mountains of mirepoix.

Over the weeks he also got to know the rhythms of the diner, the different shifts and the staff who worked them, from opening through breakfast rush, late-morning lull and lunch crush, and the afternoon stretch where so much prep happened, not only for that evening's dinner but also for the next day's breakfast.

Every day at about two o'clock, as first shift eased into second shift, Mad Dog would leave the diner and be replaced by the p.m. cook, Will.

Will was a puzzle. An imposing figure, with tattoos running from his well-muscled shoulders down to his forearms, Will moved like a shadow and rarely spoke. When he did, his voice was so soft Owen almost couldn't hear it, and with a strange accent that was hard to make out. Or so Owen thought, until he eventually realized Will wasn't calling the Chef *Chef*, as everyone else did, but *Chief*. Will and the "Chief" seemed to operate with telepathy. They hardly ever spoke a word to each other, but always seemed to know exactly what the other was doing, like two perfectly synced pieces of a fine-tuned machine. As if they'd worked together forever.

The Chef was a bit of a puzzle, too. Every Saturday evening, when Owen would tell his mom over dinner about his day at the diner ("Tell me *everything*," she would say), about the dishes they'd worked on and the things he'd learned, he would also recount the Chef's latest observations and philosophical pronouncements. She would smile and make her two-word comments: "Sounds deep," or, "Good one!" or simply, "Wow." One evening Owen said, "It's like Julia Child and Yoda got together, you know? and had a love child?"—and Mom laughed so hard she ended up snorting Chablis out her nose. (Owen laughed, too, every time he thought about it.)

If Will and the Chef were hard to figure out, Bernie, the second-shift waitress, was an open book. A short, solid, round-faced woman who laughed easily and often, Bernie came in at two to take over from Ruth—although Owen noticed that Ruth often stuck around for a while to help out. Bernie was pregnant, due in July, and though she said she planned to keep working "until the day my little man shows up," it was clear that she appreciated the help. Owen loved being around her.

Following the Chef's advice, Owen started making little mise-en-place lists, taking one dish and detailing every single ingredient and utensil he needed, and practiced building his own "batter's box" at home. As his lists multiplied, he took a blank notebook and transferred all the lists to that, and also began writing out recipes, as best as he could reproduce them. He had asked the Chef if he had any printed recipes Owen could take home with him.

"Not just yet, Owen," the Chef had replied. "That wouldn't help you right now. Recipes show you a dish from the outside in. First you have to learn them from the inside out."

Whatever *that* meant.

So Owen did his best to write them from memory.

He also kept one page in his notebook for his list of Chef's rules. The Chef hadn't said anything about a Rule Five, so Owen figured the list was probably complete as it was. Which was fine with him. Those four were plenty.

Chef's Rules

1) Taste everything.
2) Improve every dish you touch.
3) Pay attention to the little things.
4) Compose your space.

When the Chef saw Owen's notebook, with its *mise en place* lists and Owen's own scribbled versions of recipes, he nodded his approval. When he noticed the page headed "Chef's Rules," he frowned. "It's good, Owen, but remember that the rules are like recipes. It's okay to write them down, but you can't learn them from the outside in."

Actually, Owen thought, maybe he did understand that. *Do it over and over*, his father used to say when they would work on his baseball skills together. *Drill it until you don't have to think about it, until it becomes part of you.* Just like the Chef had described his *mise-en-place* lists.

Which reminded Owen: spring wasn't far off now. Baseball practice would be starting soon. For probably the hundredth time, he felt a knot of worry in his stomach. How was he going to make practice if he was stuck at the diner every Saturday?

On this particular Saturday, Owen was sitting at one of the empty booths during the late-morning lull, staring out the window. There it stood, across the street, its four stories of weathered brickwork glaring back. The cardboard and duct tape covering the big broken window had been replaced by a sheet of plywood—an ugly patch over a diseased eye.

The warehouse was an old building; supposedly it was on some sort of historic register. Decades ago, when things were booming in Mapletown, it had been the center of a thriving industry. Shoes, or fabric, or something—they'd studied it in school but Owen hadn't paid much attention. Now it was an empty shell of a place.

To Owen, it reminded him of everything he didn't like about their town.

"Must have been some rock," said Ruth, who had slipped silently into the seat next to him. "Or one serious pitching arm."

Owen stared at her, as she leaned on her elbows and peered out at the warehouse too. How did *she* know about him and the warehouse and that rock?

She looked at him with that half-sad smile. "In a diner, Owen, the waitress is the bartender. Great listener, seen it all and heard it all—and whatever's going on in town, first to know about it."

Owen's cheeks burned red. Sometimes he was so engaged in watching and learning that he was able to forget the reason he'd been sent here to the diner in the first place, or at least pretend to forget. Except it was harder when he was around the Chef, because the Chef *knew* why he was here. And now Ruth knew, too. Great.

"You know," said Ruth as she continued gazing out the window, "for years Chef has talked about raising money from the community to fix up that old place, put in sinks and walk-ins and ovens and stovetops, and convert it into a cooking school."

Owen shook his head. "And people would move to this town to go to culinary school? I don't think so. People don't move here to go to school—they move *away* from here to go to school."

Ruth frowned and pursed her lips. "Not regular culinary school, exactly. His idea was more, the school would be for teenagers. For kids from around here."

Owen looked at the monster across the street and sighed. "Personally, I can't wait to get out of this town."

They were both silent for a moment, looking out the diner window, Mapletown looking back in at them. Then Ruth said, "So Owen, can I ask you a personal question?"

Owen knew this wasn't going to have anything to do with cooking or culinary school. "Okay."

"Why'd you do it?" she said, nodding at the warehouse.

Owen stared out the window. He'd asked himself this question, many times, but he'd never really been forced to come up with an answer. Finally he shook his head and gave another sigh. "I don't know. I guess . . ."

He kept looking out the window as he talked, not daring to look at Ruth.

"I guess, the rock just felt good in my hand. I was so mad. I don't even know at what, exactly. Just, *mad*. And the rock felt like it took all that, like it sucked all that mad out of me and turned it into this ball I was holding in my hand, like if I could just throw it hard enough and hit something big enough, it would all be gone. And I would feel better."

Now he looked over at Ruth.

"So I just did. I threw it as hard as I could."

He stopped talking, remembering that moment, how exhilarating it felt to hurl that thing as far away from himself as possible, and how the explosion of shattering glass had sounded like a million pieces of silverware being dumped out of a drawer into a huge porcelain sink—and how that terrible sound had completely shattered the feeling of exhilaration and replaced it with dread.

The damage was far worse than Owen had realized. The old place was not as empty as he'd thought. When the big window burst it sent shards of glass scattering everywhere, peppering the pallets of supplies the Chef had stored there. A good deal had to be thrown out. That had turned out to be one expensive rock.

"So, did it work?"

It took a moment for Owen to register the question and refocus his eyes on Ruth. "What?"

"Throwing the balled up thing in your hand, to feel better. Did it work?"

Owen slowly shook his head, as if realizing the answer for the first time. "Nope. Sure didn't. I still felt just as bad as ever. Worse. Because now I knew I was in trouble."

Ruth was quiet for a moment. "Well," she said, "I guess *some* good came out of it. After all, it landed you here." When Owen didn't say anything, she continued. "You know, you're doing great here, Owen. You're learning so much, so fast."

Owen shrugged. "Thanks." He couldn't pull his eyes away from the bleak view across the street. "Hey," he said, "can I ask *you* a personal question?"

"Of course."

"Haven't you ever wanted to get out of here, just leave, go experience life in the big city?"

Ruth smiled. "Actually," she said, "I grew up in New York City. I've only been here in Mapletown for a little more than a decade."

That surprised Owen. He had assumed that Ruth had always lived here, her whole life. She seemed to know everyone and everything about the town. She seemed like she was part of it.

"I know," she said, as if she'd heard his thoughts. "Like I said, I'm a good listener. But I moved here the same time Will did, and for the same reason—to work with Chef."

Owen thought about what she said. "Wait—so, did you know Will *before* you moved here?"

Ruth nodded. "We both worked with Chef, in New York. At his restaurant."

"He had a *restaurant*? In *New York City*?"

"Oh, yeah," she said. "It was quite the place. Very popular, *very* successful. And we all had a blast together."

He wanted to say, "So what made him leave New York and move *here*?"—but Ruth abruptly stood up and turned back toward the counter. "Better get going," she said. "Lunch crush coming."

As he made his way back into the kitchen to see what the

Chef might want him to do, Owen thought about what Ruth had said. *You're doing great here, Owen. You're learning so fast.* He hoped that was true, and not just Ruth being nice. After all, the Chef still hadn't served a single Chef Special he'd made. Although that was something he was about to change, or so he hoped.

He had come in today with a plan.

A few hours later, when he was about to leave for the day, Owen approached the Chef and asked if he could talk to him for a moment.

"'Course," said the Chef.

"I was wondering," said Owen. "I mean, I've been coming here for a while now, and, you know, I've watched you do . . . a lot."

The Chef looked straight into Owen's eyes with his usual no-expression. "Whatever it is, Owen, just say it."

"Right," said Owen, and he took a breath. "I was wondering— do you think it would be okay, next Saturday, if I came in and opened the diner myself? I mean, with you watching, of course."

The Chef looked at him for a few long seconds that seemed like an hour. Finally, he nodded, slow and thoughtful.

"Sure, Owen. I think that would be great. See you next week, oh five hundred. On the dot."

All that week, Owen had butterflies in his stomach. He was going to have the chance to prove himself and put to the test everything he'd learned. He would show everyone that he wasn't a complete screw-up, that he *could* get his act together. That he was his father's son.

He, Owen, was going to open the diner!

8

mess

The day was a disaster.

For starters, Owen overslept. He was in the middle of a dream: standing at his school's baseball diamond in the batter's box, clutching at the handle of a three-foot-long whisk for a bat, staring downfield at Mad Dog perched on a pitcher's mound made of mirepoix and mumbling at top volume as he wound up for the pitch. The cook let fly, and suddenly a blur of three hundred eggs came zooming at Owen at a hundred miles per hour—

His eyes jerked open. He scrabbled for his watch, stared at it in horror, and tumbled out of bed.

Less than five minutes later he was on his bike, pedaling like mad. It was warm out today, and even this early in the morning everything was melting, turning the packed snow and icy paths to mud.

He reached the diner at eight minutes after five, parked and locked his bike, and ran to the front. The Chef stood waiting just outside the door. He turned when Owen reached him, panting from the ride, shirt untucked. The Chef looked closer at his face.

Owen's left eye was purple and swollen—like a boxer at the end of a bad round.

"Sorry," mumbled Owen.

Without a word, the Chef unlocked and opened the door, turned to Owen and gestured with one arm. *After you.* Owen headed for the kitchen, the Chef in tow.

All that week, Owen had played out the next hour in his head, drilling himself on the sequence over and over. But nothing went quite the way he'd rehearsed it. Rushing to make up his eight minutes, he nearly tipped over the rack of bacon as he grappled it over to the oven. Cracking his three hundred eggs took forever. His potatoes started to burn.

The Chef stayed back, watching but not interfering. "Slow down, Owen," he murmured at one point. Owen glanced frantically at the wall clock. He *couldn't* slow down. Their first customer would be walking in the door any minute!—

As he turned back to the stove he knocked over a pan of potatoes and, in a futile effort to catch them as they fell, kicked over the sani bucket, sending its water-and-bleach solution sprawling over the floor to mix with the capsized spuds.

At that moment the swinging doors pushed open and Ruth poked her head in. She took in the scene—the splattered-potato catastrophe, Owen staring in horror, and finally his swollen purple eye—and nodded.

"Nice shiner," she said. "Anyway, heads up, guys."

It was 6:00.

The next hour was torture. The Chef commandeered the cleaning of the floor and let Owen do the cooking, taking over only when the mess the boy was producing accumulated beyond tolerance levels. "Wipe your piano, son," Owen heard him murmur at least a dozen times.

I don't have TIME to wipe my piano! Owen wanted to scream, as Ruth kept slapping fresh tickets up on the pass and he struggled not to fall too far behind. Still, he dutifully grabbed that rag and wiped the piano each time, the Chef's mantra by now embedded in his brain: *Clean as you go.* "I know, I know," he muttered, "or it'll dry and be a bitch to clean later."

Fortunately they were mostly all simple orders—waffle, plate of pancakes, order of over easies, nothing fancy. Still, the Chef watched over it all ferociously, editing and revising as they went from Owen's stove to Ruth's hand, redoing individual elements on more than half Owen's plates and in some cases doing the entire plate over again. Owen did notice that a few of his breakfasts managed to slip through untouched. He would have felt more pride in that if he weren't leaving such havoc in his wake.

At seven o'clock Mad Dog appeared. He'd been briefed on the plan for Owen to open and asked to hold off coming in till seven, at which point he'd show up just in case Owen needed back-up. Which he did, badly.

Mad Dog—uncharacteristically silent—took the helm just as the breakfast rush hit its peak. He started parceling out the tickets as they appeared, most of them to himself and maybe one in eight to Owen.

Though grateful for the assist, Owen was also deeply embarrassed. Mostly, he was furious with himself. His big chance to prove himself—and he'd completely blown it.

Finally the mid-morning lull came. Some days, the rush tapered off gradually. Today the place just went empty, sudden as a gunshot. One moment they were pushing plates out the pass, and the next moment the kitchen was nearly silent.

"Good weather," the Chef commented. "People want to be outside."

Owen nodded miserably as he wiped down his piano once more and looked around the kitchen. "Sorry about all this."

"It's all right, Owen," the Chef replied. "Don't give it another thought."

"No," said Owen, "it was . . . *appalling.* I apologize. It won't happen again."

"All right," said the Chef. He nodded toward the swinging doors and added, "Let's clean." Owen followed him out to the front.

Ruth was mopping up the muddy tracks around the front door. The place looked like someone had dropped a dirty-dishes bomb. With Owen in the kitchen all morning, they'd fallen badly behind in bussing. Half the tables still needed clearing.

As the two went to work with bussing trays, the Chef said, "You know what they call this in the army, Owen?"

"What?"

The Chef cast his eye around the diner's interior, from one end to the other, then back at Owen. "The mess."

Owen stared at him.

"Joke, boy."

"Ah," said Owen, and he gave back a weak laugh.

They continued cleaning.

"Point of fact," the Chef went on, "it's not completely a joke. The word *mess,* as in *mess hall,* comes from the same root word as the *mise* in *mise-en-place.* It means, 'to put.' The mess is where you put down your meals." After a moment he added, "How the word got so messed up, I have no idea."

Owen dimly realized that the Chef was doing something he'd never seen him do before. He was rambling on, even making jokes, purely to cheer Owen up. He managed a weak grin, but it quickly faded again. "I screwed up everything, didn't I."

The Chef looked around the room again. "Not *everything*. Noticed Mad Dog gave you old Mr. Farnsworth's usual: one soft-boiled with dry toast. That came out pretty good." When Owen didn't say anything, he added, "Not feeling real jokey today, are ya."

"Sorry. I had a bad week."

The Chef nodded and looked around. The place was more or less finished; Ruth could handle the balance. He looked at Owen.

"Let's take a walk."

They put on their jackets—it was sunny and thawing, but still, April in New England was not shirt-sleeve weather—and went out front. Turning left, the Chef started walking them down the long block. Away from the warehouse, Owen noted.

"So," said the Chef after a minute. "That boy, Russ, giving you a hard time?"

Owen was stunned. How on earth did he know that? And how did he know it was Russ that he'd had the fight with, the one who gave him his big black eye? Ruth. Had to be.

In fact, Russ had been ragging on Owen about the fact that he was busy every Saturday taking "cooking lessons." They argued, and Russ called him a "mama's boy." Owen punched him. Russ punched back. Both ended up in the principal's office, their parents summoned to pick them up.

As he described what happened, he remembered the look on

Mom's face when she walked into the office to collect him. Russ's dad had been livid. Mom didn't look mad—just sad, which only made Owen feel worse.

That had been Thursday, and now Russ and Owen weren't talking.

"Which is fine with me," said Owen.

They walked on for a moment, then the Chef said, "Isn't Russ your best friend?"

"He *was*."

"He really called you a mama's boy?"

"Yep."

They walked for another moment, and then the Chef said, "Well that was pretty stupid, wasn't it."

Owen glanced at him, surprised. He hadn't quite expected the Chef to take his side on this.

"I'm not taking your side, by the way," the Chef commented. (It was scary, how the guy could read your mind.) "Just stating what's so, is all. It's not about sides."

"Yeah. Well," Owen said, "not as stupid as me. I shouldn't have punched him."

They'd reached the end of the long block, and the Chef took another left. "You're tough on yourself. Have you noticed?"

Owen shrugged.

"You know, Owen, those rules aren't just about cooking. Paying attention to the little things, composing your space—your batter's box? They're about how you *live*. A creed, you could say."

Owen looked at the ground as they walked and said nothing.

"Like Rule Two. *Improve every dish you touch*. Only it's not just about making a better sandwich. It's about raising things to a higher level.

"What if, every time you were given a task to do, any task, big or small, you stopped for a moment, took a breath, and asked your-self, 'How can I go above and beyond all reasonable expectation?' If you attacked everything you did with that *chewing-off-the-end-of-the-table* attitude? You know what you'd achieve?"

Owen shook his head.

"Anything you wanted to."

They walked another few paces in silence, and then the Chef continued.

"Or you could think of Rule Two like this: *Make the world a better place with everything you do*. Every person you interact with, having the intention that the interaction will improve their life, even if only in the smallest of ways. Leave them happier, or more appreciated, or informed about something they didn't know be-fore. Or just listened to. *That's* Rule Two: With every action you take, ask yourself, *Does this make the world a better place?* Even if it's only in your little corner of the universe. Because what you do makes a difference. Like a dash of fresh thyme in a stew, or a pinch of salt on a slice of watermelon."

They reached the end of the short block and took yet another left, heading back toward the back of the diner. After another mo-ment, the Chef continued talking.

"And that goes for yourself, too. Rule Two means you ask your-self, with every thought you let cook in your mind: *Is this thought making me a better person?* Because thinking is cooking, too."

Thinking is cooking, too? Owen would have to think about that one.

"So here's my point: don't be so tough on yourself, Owen." He paused, then added, "Let me do that."

Owen shot him a glance. Did he just make another joke? With the Chef, he could never tell.

They walked on. Owen said, "What about Rule One?"

"Rule One?"

"You said, the rules aren't just about cooking. So what about Rule One?"

The Chef stopped walking and looked at Owen, then looked around at the neighborhood. "Listen," he said. "You hear that?"

Owen listened. The sound of water jumped out at him, a river that bisected the town, running in a nearby culvert. Crows shot raucous calls at each other on the rooftops behind them. The April thaw was finally loosening winter's grip on the New England town, and the sounds of spring were everywhere.

"What do you smell?"

There was the smell of spring, too: that rich, loamy, almost sour smell of damp soil and rotting leaves just starting to emerge from under their months of snow cover.

"Okay, now I want you to imagine something with me. Let's say we just heard on the news, there's a gigantic meteor heading straight for the earth, the scientists say it's going to hit within twenty-four hours. Today, you and I are walking along, talking about mirepoix and grilled cheese. Tomorrow, kaboom. It's all gonna blow."

Owen grinned. "For real? Like the dinosaurs?" It reminded him of a movie he'd seen. "And no Bruce Willis to save the day?"

The Chef squinted. (*Full out hilarity*, thought Owen.) "No," he said, "no Bruce Willis. We're all going dinosaur. Okay?

"Now, imagine this is our last day on earth, and we all *know* this is our last day on earth. After today, you will never again hear the sound of a running stream. This is your last chance to smell the damp spring leaves. Now, how does that smell make you feel?"

Owen thought for a moment. "Sad? Angry?"

The Chef cocked his head slightly. "Angry, why?"

"Because I won't get to smell it anymore."

The Chef nodded. "I understand, and that makes sense. But don't think about the *never again* part of it, about the future or any of that. In fact, don't *think* at all. Close your eyes. Just smell that smell."

Owen closed his eyes.

"Okay? Now: This is your only chance, ever, to take in and experience that mulching-leaves scent, today, right now, right here. Tell me how that smell makes you *feel*."

Eyes still shut, Owen tried to let go of everything else and just experience the smell of the leaves, and to feel what that felt like.

"Like . . ." he began, "like I want to smell it forever. Like I want to crawl inside it and smell it from the inside. To swallow it up, gallons of it, and never let it go."

He opened his eyes again and glanced at the Chef, hoping what he'd just said didn't sound stupid.

The Chef was looking at him thoughtfully, stone still. After a moment, he nodded. "Well said, Owen. *Really* well said. That's *exactly* what it is to be a chef. You don't just want to know something with your brain. You want to know it with your skin, with your cells. You want to crawl inside how a food tastes, *swallow gallons of it and never let it go.*" He nodded once more. "Nice one." He looked around at the spring day, took a slow deep breath, and then looked at Owen again.

"Now do one more thing for me. Forget about the stream and the crows and the leaves. Close your eyes and imagine that for this last day on earth, these last moments before the meteor comes to take you and me and Bruce Willis and everyone else off to join the dinosaurs, that you could be *anywhere, anytime.* Imagine you're hearing any sounds you could possibly hear, smelling any smells, feeling any kind of sun or wind or weather on your skin. Imagine any picture, any scene you want.

"What are you hungry for? What do you want to fill your senses with, in this last and best and most perfect of all days?"

Owen closed his eyes—and in an instant he was back at the ballpark again, feeling the cool summer-evening breeze on his skin, the roasting peanuts in the air, the *crack!* of the bat and crowd's roar and surge, that big hand on his back as they watched the team they were rooting for clear the bases and sweep the inning . . .

Owen's eyes stung. He wiped them with one arm, hoping the Chef didn't notice. He would not cry.

"Always be hungry, Owen," the Chef said softly. "Don't ever let life just wash over you. Savor it—every smell, every taste, every sound, every moment, like *that*.

"Let me tell you something about the world, Owen. In too many kitchens, it's all about punching in and punching out. Pumping out a hundred covers, two hundred covers, clearing four-tops, moving people through. I've seen it. What a waste."

They were walking again now, taking their last left and nearing the diner as the Chef kept talking.

"That's not great cooking. Great cooking is about more than the food. If you want to be a great chef, of course you have to be in love with the food, with how it tastes and smells, how it feels and behaves, how it interacts and transforms. But it's not enough just to love *food*. You can't cook great food if you don't love *life*.

"*That's* Rule One, Owen. And even if you screw up or forget all the other rules, you won't go wrong if you always go back to Rule One. Taste everything."

He stopped walking, and looked directly into the boy's face.

"Taste *everything*."

They walked again, and now they were back at the diner, climbing the slate steps and opening the front door. Just before entering, the Chef spoke up once more.

"And Owen—the thing with Russ? When do you clean it?"

Owen's reply came automatically. "As you go." The Chef stood looking at him. *And . . . ?* Owen thought for a moment, then added, "Because once it dries and hardens, it's a bitch to clean later."

The Chef squinted again, then nodded. "Wipe your piano, son."

಄

Owen wiped his piano. He went over to Russ's house that evening, and the two boys talked it through. It was hard at first. Both boys had their pride wounded, and it wasn't easy to let go of that. But Russ wanted the friendship as badly as Owen did, and by the time Owen climbed back on his bike the two were once again thick as thieves.

Clean as you go, he thought as he pedaled back home. He stopped in his driveway and thought about his mom's face, picking him up at the principal's office.

But how were you supposed to clean all *this*?

Things were worse than the Chef knew, worse than even Ruth knew. His work detail at the diner had saved him from being kicked out of school, but he was still getting into trouble, more and more, in fact. His grades were sinking fast, his teachers exchanging more of those concerned, disapproving looks. The threat of flunking out hadn't exactly been brought up, at least not as far as Owen knew, but it was rumbling just over the horizon like an approaching thunderstorm: no lightning yet, but that thick electric feeling in the air.

That night Owen lay on his bed, listening. Mom's room was next door to his, and the walls didn't hide much. He didn't hear anything, and he was grateful for it. In a way, though, the silence was worse. At least before, when he'd heard her hushed weeping through the wall, he'd felt a bond. He remembered those first few September weeks, how numb he'd felt, and how just by looking at her he knew she felt the same way.

"We'll get through this, honey," she would say, and every time she did he would think, Get *through* this? What did that even mean? He didn't know what to think.

Even worse, he didn't know what to feel.

Obviously, he was supposed to feel sad, and of course he *was* sad, but if he was really honest with himself, what he really felt more was just flat-out confused.

How could his father be gone?

A *heart attack*? How was that even possible? His father was invincible, super healthy, took great care of himself. Not over-weight, never smoked or anything. He was a *coach*, for heaven's sake. When he was a young man, Mom once told Owen, they called him Thomas the Tank. He was strong as a samurai, and just fifty years old. Fifty!

The Sunday after that awful September day, the one when the woman from the school office had come to pull him out of class and bring him to the hospital, Owen and his mom were in their pew at church, sitting through a sermon on the Book of Job. He vaguely remembered the point of the sermon being that every-thing came out right as rain in the end. Better than ever. Some-thing about a "double portion." Yeah? Well what did that have to do with Owen's father? Where was *his* double portion?

In the weeks after that, Owen had heard it all. "Everything happens for a reason." "Your dad is watching over you now, son." "He wants you to make him proud." "God has a plan." A *plan*? None of it made the remotest bit of sense to Owen.

He wished people would just leave him alone.

And soon, they did. Within a month or two, the long sorrow-ful looks and brief sympathetic chats had slowed to a halt. Fall turned into winter. Now it was seven months later, and everyone else in the world had just moved on. Even his mom seemed like she was moving on—slowly, trudging by like the seasons, but moving all the same.

And Owen? He still felt just as confused as ever.

9

the invitation

The following Friday when Owen got home from school, his mom said the Chef had called their house and left a message, asking if Owen could come in the next day toward the end of the afternoon, before the dinner rush. "Let's say, sixteen thirty," he'd said. Owen did the math and figured that meant 4:30 p.m.

Wait—four thirty in the afternoon? When the place was empty? Owen's heart thudded.

The week before, when he'd messed up so bad, he'd been afraid the Chef was going to bawl him out, but instead he'd just been calm and patient. In fact, Owen had never once seen him get angry or raise his voice . . . but there was a first time for everything, right? Why else would the Chef want him to come in when no one else was around?

All his teachers thought he was a lost cause. Maybe the Chef did, too.

When he reached the diner late the following afternoon, he found Bernie sitting on the bench outside, taking a much-needed break from being on her feet. Owen parked and locked his bike, then walked over to where she sat. It wasn't quite four thirty yet. Doom could be postponed for a few more minutes.

"Okay if I join you?" he said.

Bernie laughed, patted the seat next to her, and said, "I wish you would!" Bernie instantly put Owen at ease, as she always did, and for a moment he forgot he would shortly be going inside to get yelled at.

"I used to come out here for a ciggy," she said. "I quit, though, when *he* showed up." She patted her large and growing belly. "Now I come out here just out of habit, I guess. And to take in the air."

She closed her eyes and leaned back, took a big breath in, and slowly let it out. Owen figured she was taking a long drag on her nonexistent ciggy.

"You hear that?" she said, eyes still closed and a contented smile on her face.

All Owen heard was a garbage truck lumbering down the street a few blocks away, then the squeal of its brakes as it came to a stop. And now his own heart, thudding again as he thought about his coming encounter with the Chef.

I can't wait to get out of this town, he thought.

"I love that sound," murmured Bernie.

Owen looked at her. "What sound?"

She smiled again. "Close your eyes, Owen. Listen. Hear that?"

Grudgingly, Owen closed his eyes and listened. After a moment, he realized there was a bird singing nearby. Not the clumsy racket of the crows but a songbird of some sort, warbling its little Pavarotti heart out.

"That's a mockingbird," said Bernie. "My favorite. He's always out here, singing away. And I always feel like he's singing directly to me, telling me about all the good things that are gonna happen."

She rubbed her hands around her belly, eyes still closed.

"In a few months, my little man is gonna come into the world and we're all gonna get to meet him. It's all I think about.

"I used to tell myself, *I hope my child is smart, talented, and handsome.* I would imagine him growing up to go to a wonderful college and have a brilliant career, and how proud of him I would be. As the date got closer, I started thinking, you know, it doesn't matter if he's smart and handsome and all those things, I'll just be happy if he's healthy. As the time got even closer, I thought, as long as he has ten toes and ten fingers, that's all I ask!"

She laughed, and Owen laughed with her. Then they were both quiet, listening to the mockingbird for a moment, until Bernie spoke up again.

"I have a cousin who was born deaf. She's the sweetest person. But you know what, Owen? She'll never, ever hear that bird sing. Every morning when I wake up, I think about how lucky I am. I feel the sheets against my toes, hear the rustling of leaves in the trees outside, see the sky, and I think, *Wow.* You know? The small miracles are really the big ones."

She opened her eyes and smiled. "Gets me in the right frame of mind to start my day." She looked down again at her hand on her belly. "I just pray he can see the trees and hear what you and I just heard."

Owen thought about the deaf cousin, and how she'd never, ever hear that bird sing. It struck him as so incredibly sad—and unfair. Why did things like that have to happen to people? Why did life have to be so, so . . .

He glanced up and realized Bernie was watching him.

"You know, Owen," she said, "I went through a rough patch as a kid. Not much older than you. I don't know how I would have ended up, if it weren't for an extremely kind man who took a chance on me, and gave me a job when no one else would. I'll tell you something he told me.

"'How the world treats you,' he said, 'depends mostly on where you're looking and what you're seeing. You can't wait for the world to *make* you happy. What makes you happy is the choices you make.'"

She looked at Owen again and broke into a huge Bernie grin. "I had absolutely no idea what he was talking about—and I told him so. He just laughed and said, 'That's okay. You will.'"

She hauled herself to her feet (with considerable effort) and started back toward the diner door. "Gotta go back in and get ready for the dinner rush. Thanks for listening, Owen."

After she was gone Owen stayed outside for a few minutes, alone with the sun on his face and the mockingbird's song. He frowned with concentration, and listened harder.

He kept expecting the birdsong to repeat itself, the way birds always did. But this one didn't do that. Now that he was really listening, he was struck by all the different sounds that came out of that little bird, riff after riff after riff. It seemed like it *never* repeated itself. *He's always out here, singing away*, Bernie had said. How had Owen never noticed this before?

When they both closed their eyes, Bernie had heard a song-bird. Owen had heard a garbage truck.

How the world treats you depends mostly on where you're looking and what you're seeing. It sounded to Owen like the kind of thing his father would've said.

Pay attention to the little things, he thought. *When you do, the big things tend to take care of themselves.* Or as Bernie put it, *The small miracles are really the big ones.* Thinking about Bernie, hoping and praying for ten fingers and ten toes on her "little man," made him smile.

Owen wanted to stay on that bench, listening to the songbird instead of the garbage truck, thinking about everything Bernie said. He wished he could sit there in the April sun forever.

But he couldn't. It was time to go inside and face the music.

He found the Chef sitting in his little office, pencil in hand, bent over the month's bookkeeping. Though the door was open (as it always was), the Chef didn't seem to notice him standing there. He knocked lightly.

The Chef looked up. For a moment, he didn't say anything. Then he nodded down at his bookkeeping.

"I've been keeping a tally of the hours you've worked, Owen. As of last week, you've worked off the damage. Done. We're square. No more indentured servitude. In other words, your Saturdays are yours again."

Owen was so surprised he couldn't speak.

"I want to thank you," the Chef said. "You've done good work. I've appreciated having you here. We all have." He went back to his bookkeeping, checking off one column at a time with his pencil as he went through the figures.

Owen stood there in the doorway, not knowing how to react or what to do. That was *it?*

The Chef looked up again. "That's it. You're free to go."

Owen felt like laughing out loud with relief. Not only was he *not* going to get yelled at, but he'd just gotten the best news of the year. *Saturdays!* Baseball was his life—and he wasn't going to miss it after all! No more taunting from his friends. No more grief from Russ. And this year, Owen was going to make starting pitcher, he just knew it.

But . . .

But what?

To his surprise, he wasn't only feeling relieved, he was also

feeling sort of torn. Like he'd been freed, but also like he'd been
. . . fired, or something. He felt—well, what *was* it exactly? Angry?
No, more like, let down.

Owen couldn't find the word for what he felt, but if he had, it
would have been: *loss.*

The Chef continued at his bookkeeping.

Owen took a step out of the office, then stopped and turned.
"Chef?"

The Chef looked up. "Yes, Owen?"

"Is there, uh, is there any way I could, maybe . . . ?"

"Could what, Owen?"

Owen wasn't sure what he wanted to ask. "Never mind." He
stepped out of the office and quietly closed the door behind him.

After the boy was gone, the Chef looked up at the closed door. For
a long moment, he didn't move, just gazed at the door, thinking.
His heart felt heavy. He took a long, slow breath, then he put his
head down again and continued at his work.

A minute later there was a light knock at the door. The Chef
looked up again. "Come in," he called out.

The door cracked open, and the boy stuck his head in again.

"Come in, Owen," said the Chef quietly.

Owen opened the door all the way and stepped back inside the
little office. "I was wondering . . . is there any way I could keep
working here? Helping out, whatever?"

The Chef put his pencil down and closed his books. He sat
back in his chair and looked at the boy. Then he gestured toward
the little folding chair. The boy sat.

"As a matter of fact, since you ask, there's something I'd like to propose."

There was an event coming up at the end of May, the Chef explained, a big deal, at the big auditorium downtown, with a banquet and awards and speeches, that sort of thing. The Chef and Will were going to be in charge of the food preparation. There would be a dozen or so, working in the big kitchen there on site, not counting the small army of servers working the front of the house.

He wanted to invite Owen to be part of the team that put on the banquet.

Owen's heart, which had been thudding with dread only twenty minutes earlier, was now hammering with excitement. A banquet!

"What – what do you want *me* to do?" he stammered. He realized that now he felt torn again. This was a totally exciting idea—but did it mean he would lose his weekends after all, and completely miss out on the baseball season?

"For now," the Chef continued, "I thought you could join me in trying out recipes, help put the menu together. Maybe we could meet together in the afternoon, on Sundays. Saturdays, I really ought to be here at work."

Owen nearly let out a whoop of relief. He was going to help put on the big banquet—*and* he still had his Saturdays!

"We can work out of my own kitchen at home," the Chef was saying, "so we don't have the distractions of the diner. Will and Mad Dog'll manage just fine without us."

Without *us*, he'd said. They'd manage just fine without *us*. Owen flushed with pride at being included in that sentence. He got up to leave—but the Chef motioned him to sit again.

"Hang on another moment," said the Chef. "I have something for you." He reached down to a shelf behind his desk, retrieved something and placed it on the desk in front of Owen.

It was a rock.

No, not *a* rock. It was *the* rock.

"That's yours," said the Chef, his eyes on Owen's face. "Keep it if you want. If I were you, I would."

Owen's cheeks burned; he kept his eyes down. "To remind myself what a jerk I was?"

"No, Owen. To remind yourself of the choices you have."

Owen paused. "Choices?"

"Owen," said the Chef. Now Owen looked up, and the Chef continued. "You can throw a rock. You can throw a punch. You can throw a baseball. Choices."

Owen nodded and picked up the rock, wrestling it into his pocket.

"You can't control the wind," added the Chef, "but you *can* control the sail."

∽

When he got home Owen told his mom all about the banquet and about him being part of the preparations over the weeks ahead. He was afraid she'd think it was crazy, that he was taking on too much, with baseball season starting and his schoolwork still struggling. But she just nodded, as if she'd been expecting this news, and said, "I'm so proud of you for doing this, honey."

Then she added, "I can't wait."

It took a moment for the comment to sink in. "Hang on," he said. "You mean, *you'll* be there?"

She smiled. "Are you kidding? I wouldn't miss it for the world." She reached out, tucked a wisp of flyaway hair back behind his ear, then took a step back to look at him. "Not for the world."

10

olympic gold

It was a good five miles from Owen's house to where the Chef lived and his mom had offered to drive him over, but the next day proved to be the kind of late-April Sunday that was custom built for a long bike ride: warm, sunny, clear as polished glass. As Owen neared the Chef's address he biked past two parks, a large pond, and beautiful neighborhoods with tree-lined sidewalks.

Then he was there. He stopped, looked up, and whistled. The Chef's house was not as big as some he'd passed, but it sure looked big to Owen. He parked his bike, walked up to the huge front door, and knocked lightly. The Chef had said it'd be open and to come right in, but he felt funny doing so without knocking first.

No answer. He tried the knob; it was open. He stepped inside. Standing in the front vestibule, he saw a large formal dining room on the right, and to the left, two big glass doors opening onto what looked like a study or small office.

"Straight back!" the Chef's voice came down the long hall directly in front of him. Owen walked toward the voice, feeling like he was walking through a museum, and soon reached the kitchen.

It was breathtaking.

Owen's only experience of kitchens other than those in his and his friends' homes was the diner's kitchen, which always felt close and crowded. This was the total opposite. Spacious, open, tons of sunlight pouring in through a thousand windows. And everything—from the six-burner stove and polished steel griddle, to the oversize double-door brushed steel fridge, to the wall-mounted double ovens and deep stainless steel sinks where the Chef now stood—everything looked sparkling and practically brand new.

The big windows behind the double sink looked out onto a large backyard, lined with row after row of garden, a woman sitting cross-legged in the grass, pulling weeds.

"I've never seen Mrs. Kellaway happier than with her toes in the dirt and her hands pulling weeds," said the Chef.

There was an odd smell in the kitchen that Owen couldn't quite identify: slightly smoky, slightly gamey, slightly rich. He thought about the Christmas carol, *chestnuts roasting on an open fire* . . . but whatever this was, it definitely wasn't chestnuts.

"Let's cook," said the Chef.

On the island in the center of the kitchen he had lined up a plate, a bowl, a clear plastic bucket, and a lemon.

He pointed at the plate, which held a small mound of ground chicken. "One pound." Then he pointed to the bowl, filled with a medium-dice mirepoix. "One pound." Then at the bucket: "Chicken stock, one gallon." Finally he pointed to the lemon: "Acid."

He looked at Owen. "Can you get me the whites of three eggs?"

Owen went to the monster-sized fridge, took out three eggs, and cracked them over a large bowl the Chef handed him, separating out the yolks and setting those aside in a coffee cup.

The Chef whisked the egg whites until they started to froth, added the ground chicken and mirepoix and mixed it all together, then sliced the lemon into quarter-wedges and squeezed all their juice into the bowl. He added a few herbs—Owen identified a bay leaf, some crushed garlic, thyme and rosemary, and a few peppercorns—then placed the whole mixture into an empty soup pot sitting on a burner, poured in the gallon of stock, switched on the fire under it, and turned to Owen.

"Your job," he said. "Stir. Not constantly, just enough so those egg whites don't scramble."

Owen had no idea what they were making.

"Now," said the Chef, "let's talk about *the beginning of things*."

"Have you noticed, when you peel carrots, where the peels go?"

Owen had wondered about that. They were always tossing their peels and vegetable scraps into a tub at the back of the counter. He assumed it all got thrown out at the end of the day. But then, why collect it all day, why not just toss it in the garbage as they go?

"Nothing useful goes in the garbage, Owen. All our mirepoix trim, the bones from roasting chickens, fish heads and racks, it all goes into our stock. One day, it's beef stock, the next day fish, after that chicken or turkey . . . we make all our stock ourselves, and we *always* have stock going.

"Stock is the foundation. If you don't start with good stock, you're lost. And good stock, strong flavorful stock, starts with bones." He opened the oven door to give Owen a peek.

That's what that smell was! The Chef was roasting beef bones in his oven.

"These have been roasting for about an hour. Let's paint them."

He took the roasting pan out of the oven, set it on the counter, and rubbed the bones with tomato paste, then slid it all back into the oven.

"We'll get that tomato paste slightly toasted so it opens up, gets that acid around the pan, and starts to caramelize, then pull the bones out into a stock pot, cover them with water, and bring them up to just under a boil—you never let it actually boil, and *never* stir it, or you'll get a cloudy mess. Then you gently simmer . . ."

He went on to describe the whole process. Those bones would cook for four or five hours (for really large batches, sometimes even overnight) and the Chef would keep going back to the pot and skimming off the fat, burnt bits, and other stuff that floated to the surface. ("If you don't skim it, the stock can't breathe," he added, "and it chokes like a stagnant pond.") An hour or so before it was finished, he would add in pan-roasted mirepoix, deglazing its roasting pan with water and adding that, too, and finish it with some basic seasoning, bay leaf and peppercorns, maybe rosemary and thyme, then finally strain it.

As the Chef talked, Owen kept periodically stirring the mysterious egg-whites pot.

"That's for beef stock," the Chef went on. "For chicken or fish stock, you don't roast the bones, just skip that step and go right to the simmer. And you don't cook them so long, either, which of course means you dice your mirepoix finer. Fish stock takes maybe forty-five to fifty minutes; after that its delicate bones will be exhausted. For chicken stock, it's more like two to three hours. But you can't put an exact time on it. You have to feel it, smell it, baby it. . . ."

Suddenly Owen felt something shift in the pot he was stirring.

The Chef reached over and gently tugged Owen's arm up and

out of the pot.

"Watch," he said.

As they both stared into the pot, the chicken-mirepoix–egg white mixture changed. It all began pulling up to the surface and forming something that looked almost like the Styrofoam paddle-boards Owen remembered using when he was first learning to swim.

Owen looked at the Chef.

"Alchemy," said the Chef. "It's called a 'raft.' When it hits exactly one hundred twenty degrees in there, the egg whites coagulate and form a fine mesh, pulling everything up with them, from the bottom to the top. Here, look."

He poked gently at the solidified mixture with a wooden spoon. It rocked slightly on the liquid's surface, like . . . well, like a *raft*.

"From this point on you don't touch it. We'll bring it up to a bit below boiling—you *never* let it boil—and let it gently simmer."

For the next hour, the Chef walked Owen through the preparation of a hearty white bean soup (chicken and chorizo! garlic and oregano! escarole and shallots! insanely delicious) that he called "my Landreaux special," and then he turned to Owen, held up both index fingers, and announced:

"And now, the miracle. *Fresh consommé.*"

He returned to the steeping pot with its egg-white raft, and slowly, carefully, pushed a big ladle down in along the edge. Ladle by ladle, he scooped out the liquid and poured it through a China cap (that big conical strainer) lined with a coffee filter into a fresh, clean pot.

The crystal clear broth reminded Owen of one summer when he and his parents stayed at a little cabin in Maine. Standing at the end of the dock on a crisp, cold morning, they could see fifteen feet down to the bottom of the lake as if it were through glass. He described the memory, and the Chef nodded.

"I was in a competition once, in Europe," said the Chef. "I'd made a big pot of beef consommé. The judge walked over, fished a pfennig out of his pocket, peered close at it, then tossed it in the pot. 'Vot iss za date on za coin?' he said. I looked into the pot for a moment, then turned to him and said, '1965.' He nodded and walked on to the next contestant."

Owen looked puzzled. "What was so important about the date?"

"If I'd failed to read the numbers on the coin," the Chef said, "I would have been out of the competition. It would have meant my broth wasn't clear enough." He shook his head. "That guy was *old school.*" It sounded to Owen like he meant it as a compliment.

The Chef dipped a tablespoon into the clear broth and passed it to Owen to taste.

Owen expected something tepid and bland—the stuff looked like nothing more than colored water, after all—and was not prepared for the explosion of sensation that hit the roof of his mouth. He turned a wide-eyed stare to the Chef.

"What did you *do?*" His lips were practically stuck together from the richness of the broth. "That's . . . unbelievable!"

"Isn't it?" said the Chef. "How can something so clear be packed with so much flavor?" He tasted it, too, and closed his eyes for a moment, then smacked his lips a few times and sighed. "That, Owen, is consommé. A completely clear broth—no fat, no particles of anything, just incredibly rich, powerful flavor. And as far as what I did? You saw the whole thing. And you know where it began."

He looked at Owen, who stopped and thought for a moment.

"Oh," said Owen. "*The beginning of things.*"

It started with good stock.

The Chef glanced at the wall clock: nearly time for Owen to leave. He took off his apron and headed for the front hallway. "C'mon," he said. "There's something I want to show you."

Owen followed the Chef toward the front of the house, where they took a right through the double glass doors and stepped into the Chef's private office.

On the far side of the room, a small computer sat on a little desk, surrounded by stacks of papers. A handful of picture frames dotted the walls: an old snapshot of some men in uniform, a few framed documents that looked like certificates or awards, in languages Owen couldn't read—and some photos of the Chef standing with a few celebrity chefs Owen recognized from TV! *Holy cow*, he thought. How did the Chef know *them*?

Otherwise the room was fairly bare—except for the boxes piled up along every wall. The place was jammed with cardboard cartons.

Owen walked over to the right to get a closer look at the first frame. Under the glass, seven bronze medals were arranged around a card in the center with printed descriptions of each one.

Portland, ME • 1974 • Best of Show
Portland, ME • 1975 • Most Integrated Piece of Show
NE Regionals • 1980 • Buffet Display
Austrian Chef's Association • 1978 • Special Award
Boston Hotel Show • 1979 • Centerpiece
NE Regionals • 1980 • Centerpiece
NE Regionals • 1975 • Medal of Honor

"Wow, these are cool!" mused Owen as he read the card. He glanced down at the carton at his feet and noticed there were more framed pieces stacked up inside there. Same with the one next to it, and the one next to that. "Why is everything all boxed up?"

"Well," the Chef scratched his chin. "When we left New York and moved up here, I just never got around to hanging up the rest of it."

"Wow," said Owen again. He looked down at the one by his feet. "Is it okay if I look?"

The Chef shrugged, which Owen took to mean, *Sure, go ahead.* He pulled out one frame.

Internationale Kochkunst-Ausstellung
OLYMPIADE DER KÖCHE
ACF Regional Team

"Wait," said Owen. "Olympiade? Is that like, the Olympics? There's cooking in the *Olympics*?"

The Chef nodded. "The Culinary Olympics. They hold it every four years, just like the sports Olympics, except it's always in Germany. Teams come to compete from all over the world, including a bunch from the U.S. The ACF is the most—"

"Ohmigosh, Chef," Owen burst in, "are these really *gold*?" He held up a framed plaque with three polished gold-plated medals that reflected the afternoon sunlight like mirrors. "They *are*!" He looked up at the Chef, his eyes wide. "You guys won *gold medals*? You were the *best in the world*?"

The Chef shrugged again. "We went, we saw, we cooked."

"Are you *serious*?!" Owen dug through the box some more and found more gold medals from other international competitions—

from Switzerland, Ireland, Luxembourg, Singapore, England, and more.

Owen kneeled down by the box and dug deeper, coming up with a framed photo of seven men and women, all of them grinning, all holding up their gold medals. None looked older than thirty, and the one in front, clearly their captain and clearly the youngest of the group by far, was the Chef.

"My first Olympic team," the Chef said quietly.

Owen was still on his knees, staring dumbfounded at the gold medals. "You were *best in the world*!" he repeated. "Man, you kicked their butts! You beat *everyone*!"

"True," said the Chef. "But competition isn't about beating the other guy. The other guy isn't your enemy, Owen. The other guy is your whetstone, the hard surface that sharpens you. The point isn't to make the other team lose, it's about sharpening yourself. Winning is what happens in the process."

Owen heard barely a word of this. "I don't get it," he said. "All these gold medals, *Olympic* gold medals. How come they're stuffed away in a box—and all you've got on the wall is some old bronze medals from local events?"

The Chef walked over to the desk against the far wall and settled into his desk chair.

"Those bronze were the first medals I ever got, my first few times out to the different competitions. I wasn't ready for the Olympics. I wanted to be, but I wasn't, not yet. But those first few achievements . . . they may not be the most prestigious, or the most famous. But they were the ones I worked the hardest for, and they mean the most."

He mused quietly for a moment, then said, "And you know, that's how it usually is. The world may applaud when they see you make it across the finish line, Owen. What they don't see is how hard it was just to get to the starting line.

"Those bronze medals were my starting line. The determination, the blood, sweat, and tears it took to get there, that's something I don't ever want to forget. They were my foundation. My stock. And all the gold?" The Chef waved one hand in a gesture that said, *Eh*. "That's just how it played it out from there."

Owen finally tore himself away from the cartons of Olympic medals and memorabilia, and moved on to the next wall hanging. It was the largest in the room. In the center was an eagle wearing a striped shield and clutching a bunch of arrows with one talon, a leafy branch in the other. It was bordered by a circle of tiny stars, and around that another circle with letters that said . . .

"The *President* of the *United States*? Whoa! I can see why you'd want to hang *that* one."

"To tell you the truth, Owen, I hung that one there because it's the biggest award I have."

Owen stared at it. "No kidding. The *White House*! It doesn't get any bigger than that!" He noticed the Chef squinting, big time, and thought, *What's so funny?*

"No," said the Chef, "I mean, the *biggest*." He got out of his chair, came over, took hold of the White House award frame with both hands and carefully lifted it down off the wall. Behind where it had hung there was a large hole.

Owen threw a puzzled glance at the Chef, and could have sworn he looked almost embarrassed.

"When we got here, the movers had left this big hole in the wall. I needed something to cover it up. This was my biggest award." He rubbed his chin again. "Guess I never did get around to fixing that hole." He looked over at Owen. "Oops."

Owen was barely listening. He had already started into the next box over, and now pulled out a series of three framed photos, each one of a different former U.S. president shaking hands with the Chef, each signed with a personal note thanking the Chef for his great work on the behalf of others.

Three photos—signed by three presidents!

"Why didn't you *tell* me about this stuff? This is totally amazing! Does everyone else at the diner know about all this? They must!" He felt like he was babbling, but he couldn't stop. "I mean, holy cow, Chef, you're . . . you're *famous!*"

Owen's mind was ablaze. Famous!

He suddenly felt a fierce conviction, deep in his gut: If he were famous, like the Chef had obviously been, it would totally change his life. He wouldn't get picked on by his teachers and teased by his friends. He wouldn't always feel like fighting.

If he were famous, the hurting would stop.

The Chef gently took the photos from him and placed them back in the box, then walked Owen with him over to the desk, pulled up another chair, and sat them both down. "That's what I wanted to talk to you about, Owen. More or less."

He paused, as if trying to decide how to phrase it.

"I haven't told you about Rule Five yet, have I."

"At the restaurant," he began (Owen knew immediately that he was talking not about the diner but about his place in New York, the one Ruth had mentioned) "there were times—many times—when I was asked to come out of the kitchen and into the dining room to take a bow. To come talk to the guests about one particular dish or another, or even wow them with a quick demonstration of something impressive.

"I almost always declined. Because that evening was not about the chef or his achievements, it was about the people and the event they were celebrating—the wedding party, the anniversary, the business meeting, or whatever it was.

"Don't get me wrong, Owen. When I help create an amazing meal, I'm proud of what we do. But it isn't about me.

"This is a mistake I've seen so many chefs make, even some of the biggest. Thinking that their successes were about them, about their own skill and achievements. And it never is. It's about the experience of making great food, and even more, about who your people become in the process. Forget about grabbing the limelight—it's about pushing *them* forward, building *their* brand, helping them hone *their* skills, shining the light on *them*.

"In the Olympic teams they always said, 'There is no greater high than the honor and privilege of representing your country.' But there is: helping someone else discover their own greatness. Bringing out the true flavors of a person, you could say. Helping them serve themselves to the world.

"No," he said, "there's no better feeling than that."

He paused for a moment, looking at Owen. It seemed to Owen that he was thinking hard about something, something important, though Owen had no idea what. And unlike a few minutes earlier, when he was pawing through the cartons, Owen was now listening to every word.

"This thing we do, Owen, as chefs? There's a reason they call it 'the hospitality business,' and not 'the food business.' Because it's not really about the food. Hospitality means 'hosting.' Serving. When you *host* someone, that means you put them first. That's why you're there: for *them*.

"Fame is a tricky thing, Owen. Not a bad thing. But tricky. There are two paths to fame. You can get to the top by climbing over other people. It works, but it's ugly, and sooner or later you'll fall back down. Or, you can focus on building other people up—and they'll carry you to the top.

"And that, Owen, that's Rule Five. Build your people. *Build your team.*

"You can be the most brilliant kitchen technician in the world. But a chef who can't build people has no career in front of him. People are what it's about."

He turned his chair to look at the wall behind him. Owen followed his gaze to the frame that hung directly over the Chef's desk. It looked like a handwritten letter.

Owen stared first at the letter, then at the Chef. "Don't tell me. Is that a handwritten letter from the president?"

The Chef turned and glanced at the letter. "Better than that."

Better than a letter from the *president?* Owen stepped closer and read the name signed at the bottom.

Julie Landreaux

He looked back at the Chef. "Who is Julie Landreaux?"

"This was, oh, nearly thirty years ago," the Chef began. "Big flood, a bad one, out in the Midwest. A lot of houses were destroyed. Some people died. A whole lot more survived but lost everything they had.

"I got the call at three in the morning. Could I come out there and feed the rescue workers? Maybe help feed some of the people they were rescuing?

"I left a skeleton crew to run the restaurant, took my core staff with me, and we hopped on a plane to head out there and help with the disaster relief. We were there for five days. Don't think I slept the whole time. Set up at the big shelter there, cooked for a few hundred survivors and their families." He nodded at the letter.

"Julie was one of them."

He nodded back in the direction of the kitchen. "That consommé I just showed you? That's one of the neatest stunts in a chef's bag of tricks you'll ever see. But the soup we made for those people?" He gazed at the letter. "Now *that* was a life-changing cooking experience."

Owen looked at the name at the bottom of the letter again, and this time he made the connection. "Your 'Landreaux special,'" he said.

The Chef swiveled his gaze back to Owen. "I wanted you to know the truth about what it means to be a chef.

"Being a chef is hard. It's one of the toughest occupations to break even or make back your investment. Restaurants are always going out of business. And running a restaurant means brutal hours. It can be . . ." he paused, went silent for a long moment, then looked at Owen again. "It can be tough on a family. Okay?

"But this isn't just a profession. It's a calling. We change lives.

"Maybe your neighbor is an electrician, or a plumber, or a math teacher. All good and noble professions, but you never go, 'Hey, Frank, why don't you come over on Saturday, and we'll change some light sockets, or unplug a drain, or do some equations.'

"But chefs? Our work is different. Our work is like communion, breaking bread together, sharing life together. A chef's life is about bringing people joy. You're feeding people, nourishing their cells, and that's as primal as it gets. Only you're not just feeding their bodies. You feed them beauty, too. You feed them . . . something elevated, something that touches greatness."

He nodded at the letter. *Go ahead, read it.*

Owen read it out loud.

Dear Chef Kellaway,

I want to thank you for what you and your staff did for my family. We lost everything. I don't think most people know what that's like. But you and your team showed us that we hadn't lost everything, after all.

My daughter asked me why I cried when I started writing this letter. "Mom, it was just soup," she said. But it wasn't just soup to us. It was hope. It said someone cared about us, that we mattered. It was _love_.

Anyway, I just wanted to thank you again for the kindness you all showed. God bless you and your family, and everyone on your team. Sincerely,

Julie Landreaux

When he got to the end, Owen had a hard time finishing because of the lump in his throat.

It wasn't just soup to us. It was love.

For one timeless moment he was no longer in the Chef's home office . . . he was back in his kitchen at home, a boy of seven or eight, watching his father make The Recipe.

The secret ingredient isn't anything in *the pancakes, Owen. The secret ingredient is who you're making them for.*

The Chef's voice brought him back to where he was, standing at the little desk, looking at the framed letter on the wall.

"*This* is what I wanted to show you," said the Chef. "I treasure this note more than all the medals and awards, the fame and the photos.

"*This*, Owen. This is my Olympic Gold."

A knock came at the office door. They both turned to find the woman the Chef had called "Mrs. Kellaway" standing in the doorway, beaming at them.

When she saw Owen's face, she looked almost startled, like there was something about seeing him there that surprised her. She glanced briefly at the Chef, and Owen thought some kind of wordless communication passed between the two of them. He wondered what it meant. An instant later her face lit right back up again in a smile as warm as fresh-baked bread.

"So you're Owen!" she said, coming toward him and (to his great surprise) enveloping him in a big hug, then holding him back with both hands on his arms and looking into his face. "It's so, so nice to have you here! John has said the nicest things about you."

"She's lying," the Chef said immediately. Owen looked at him. No expression on his face, as usual.

"Oh, John, stop it!" his wife said and she swatted him on the arm.

"I said nothing nice whatsoever," he continued, as if she hadn't spoken.

She shushed him and leaned toward Owen. "He said you were one of the brightest and most promising young students he'd ever worked with." She looked back at the Chef over her shoulder. "That's what you *said*, John."

The Chef gave a noncommittal shrug.

Owen was so embarrassed he didn't know what to do, so he just nodded and said, "Thank you, Mrs. Kellaway, I have to go," and shot out the door.

Had the Chef really said those things about him? Or was she just being nice?

❧

As the boy rode off down the street the two stood in the doorway, watching him. Louise Kellaway murmured, "He looks so much like Thomas, doesn't he?"

Her husband nodded. "That he does," he said. "That he does."

They stayed at the door, watching, as the boy shrank to the end of the street and disappeared around a corner.

"Have you told him?" she said quietly. When the Chef said nothing, she turned to look at him. "John. You can't keep him in the dark. It's not fair to the boy."

The Chef sighed. "I know. And I will. I just want to give him a little more time."

She dropped her chin and peered at him over the top of her glasses. "Give *him* a little more time?"

Avoiding her gaze, the Chef turned back into the house. "I'll talk to him, Louise. Soon."

11

excellence

The next day after school, Owen showed up at the diner again. The place was nearly empty, just a few late lunchers having long conversations in the last few booths, Ruth behind the counter. Technically speaking, her shift ended at two thirty, but these days she often stayed on an extra hour or two to give Bernie a break. Bernie never complained about it, but everyone could see that the bigger her belly grew, the more her back ached, and she was clearly grateful for the assist.

Owen took a seat at the first stool, what he'd come to think of as "his" stool.

"Chef's not here, you know," said Ruth.

"That's okay," replied Owen. "He wasn't expecting me or anything. I've just got a few hours free, and I wondered if maybe there's anything I could do to help out?"

It looked like he was going to be a part of this banquet team, along with Ruth, Mad Dog, and Will. Coming to the diner to help out, he figured, was something like going out to the batting cage on your own for extra practice. If he was going to do anything

other than just get in the way once that banquet was actually happening, it might not be a bad idea to put in some batting practice
now.

And over the next four or five weeks, he did. He came by
nearly every weekday after school, on those days he didn't have
practice. In addition to helping serve and clear tables, he also got
into the kitchen to help Will prep for dinner—setting up the dinner racks, prepping garnishes, and the rest. The late afternoons
were really slow out front anyway and there wasn't much to do
until the dinner rush. He liked learning the details of prep, and he
was growing to love the rhythms of the place.

Every so often, he got the chance to try his hand at a Chef
Special again. The afternoon hours were fairly slow, not like Saturdays, and the demand was slight. Still, at least one or two customers would usually drop by for a late lunch and order the Special,
and Owen would grab it if he could. He kept hoping his efforts
would pass the test and actually be served out front.

To be completely honest with himself, there was also one more
reason he wanted to keep hanging out at the diner.

He'd thought a good deal about everything the Chef had said
that day at his home, looking at his awards. In fact, it had kind of
gnawed at him.

For one thing, they were in the middle of baseball tryouts.
Owen wanted more than anything to make starting pitcher this
year, which put him in direct competition with a few other kids.
He would do anything to beat those guys. Which had made him
think about the Chef's comments on competition. "Forget about
grabbing the limelight," the Chef had said, "push *them* forward,
shine the light on *them*." How was he supposed to do that, and still
make starting pitcher? How was he supposed to do that, and still
get what he wanted?

After that first visit to the Chef's home, Owen had sworn to himself that someday, he would become famous like the Chef had been. But the Chef himself didn't seem to think his own fame was any big deal, like it didn't matter at all. Owen didn't understand that. How could it possibly *not* matter?

Most of all, though, what the Chef said gnawed at him because of that phrase he'd used, his Rule Five:

Build your team.

Because those three words were exactly—*exactly*—what his father had always said. And not just to Owen, but to every student at Mapletown High School who'd ever been on one of his teams. *Build your team.* That was "Coach Devon's cardinal rule." He was famous for it. Had the Chef somehow gotten that from his father? Owen couldn't see how. They didn't even know each other. Did they?

Owen knew his father had played ball in college, and was pretty good, too, before going into the army. He was pretty sure that after the army he'd worked in a kitchen himself for a while, professionally, before becoming a coach. Could his father and the Chef have crossed paths at some point? He figured it was possible. But his parents had never talked about those years, at least not when Owen was around.

Ever since that conversation with Ruth about New York, Owen had been curious about the Chef's history and background. Now, after seeing all those awards, learning about the Olympics and the White House and everything, and with that unasked question about the Chef and his father, that curiosity was burning like a fever.

But it wasn't easy to get any answers at the diner, either. The Chef didn't like to talk about himself much. Will didn't like to talk, period, as far as Owen could see. Even spending time with him in the kitchen during the afternoon lull, it was a rare thing to engage him in a comment or two beyond explaining something about whatever dinner prep they were doing. There was only so much he could get Ruth to say, especially since she often left for the day soon after he arrived. And while Bernie was probably the easiest person in the world to talk to, Owen didn't think she'd been part of the New York experience, and had no reason to think she'd have any answers for him.

Meanwhile, every Sunday he biked over to the Chef's house, and they worked on dish after dish after dish. In the process Owen got a crash course in all the essentials of great cooking. Every session was almost like a seminar, like the extensive lesson on stock and soups he'd learned that first Sunday.

The next Sunday, the Chef taught Owen about the Big Five.

"There are five basic cooking techniques," he said, when they gathered around the sunlit island over cups of hot tea. "There's braising, sautéing, frying, roasting, and poaching. Once you master these five, in theory you can cook *anything*." And he proceeded to walk Owen through all five.

Another Sunday, the topic was Ratios.

Owen had watched Will put together half a dozen quiches one day at the diner, and he tried to duplicate the recipe at home with a single pie for him and his mom—but it had flopped. When he pulled his solo quiche out of the oven, the top was totally browned, yet the inside was still soupy.

"The thing hadn't set," he told the Chef, "so it was impossible to slice—but if I cooked it any more, it would have burned."

"Do you know what your ratio was?" said the Chef.

Owen had no idea what he meant.

"You've got to have a ratio. There are all kinds of quiche reci-pes—some with milk, some with cream and milk, some with whole eggs plus yolks, others with just eggs. But regardless of the details, you need a basic custard ratio in your head that you know works. The ratio for a good custard is seven to one: seven eggs to one quart of milk."

"Seven eggs to one quart," repeated Owen. "Got it."

"Remember how we started that consommé?"

Owen remembered, all right. "Ground chicken: one pound. Mirepoix: one pound. Stock: one gallon. Egg whites: three."

The Chef nodded. "And you can use that ratio to make any kind of consommé you want—beef, duck, pheasant, prawns, you name it: one pound, one pound, one gallon, three.

"For a chef, ratios are golden. Once you know your basic ratios, you can adapt virtually any recipe to any scale or variation. For ex-ample, your basic vinaigrette is three to one, oil to vinegar. Doesn't matter what kind of vinegar, what herbs or Parmesan/Romano or spices or other seasonings you add, it's going to be three to one. For bread—"

"Chef," Owen said, "would it be okay to write this down?"

"Yes," said the Chef as he slipped a pad of paper and pen out of an unseen drawer in the island and passed them over to Owen. "*This*, you definitely want to write down. So where was I?"

Owen had just jotted down:

Quiche   7:1 – eggs to qt milk
Vinaigrette   3:1 – oil to vinegar
Bread

"You're on bread," he said.

"Right. Bread is five to three, flour to water. Pie dough is three to two to one, flour to fat to water. Cookie dough? One to two to three, sugar to fat to flour—or, for a sweeter cookie, four to five to six. Pasta? Three to two, flour to egg. Roux, for thickening a sauce, is one to one, flour to butter or whatever fat you're using. Mayonnaise is *twenty* to one, oil to liquid—plus yolk, about one per cup of mayo. Sausage: three to one, lean meat to fat."

Owen was scribbling as fast as he could. His list now included:

Quiche	7:1 – eggs to qt milk
Vinaigrette	3:1 – oil to vinegar
Bread	5:3 – flour to H_2O
Pie dough	3:2:1 – flour/fat/H_2O
Cookie dough	1:2:3 or 4:5:6 – sugar/fat/flour
Pasta	3:2 – flour to egg
Roux	1:1 – flour to fat
Mayo	20:1 – oil to liquid + 1 yolk/cup
Sausage	3:1 – lean to fat

"Knowing your ratios," the Chef was saying, "frees you from the tyranny of recipes. Once you know your ratios, you can do anything." And they proceeded to make each of those ratios into a delicious dish.

On still another Sunday the Chef announced that their topic was going to be Using Your Nose and Ears.

They started out with a prime rib. When Owen arrived, the Chef had a big standing rib roast sitting out on a plate on the counter.

"I took it out nearly an hour ago," he said. "If you put it cold right into a hot oven it'll tense up, just like your muscles tense up when you're about to throw a pitch. So first thing you do is take it out and let it rest. That's one of the biggest secrets to a good, moist roast, and it's pretty much true for any protein—a steak, chicken thigh, piece of salmon on the grill. Let it rest at room temperature *before* you cook it, just like you do after it's cooked."

He put the meat in a roasting pan and slipped it into one of his ovens, already heated to a blazing 450°—that hot to start, he explained, to create a good sear that locked in the juices, just like starting a filet in a hot skillet. Before long, he would turn it down to slow-roast.

"The question is, how do we know when it's time to turn it down?"

Owen looked at the wall clock. "You time it?" he ventured, already knowing the right answer wouldn't be that obvious.

"You *listen*, Owen. You turn it down when it starts to talk to you. The meat will start to sizzle, just like your filet in the skillet, and then you can turn it down to, say, 250°, finish it low and slow so it can cook perfectly all the way through."

"How long will that take?"

The Chef looked at Owen, then back at the roast. "We'll know."

For the next few hours he walked Owen through a dozen examples of cooking by smell, sound, and feel. He even had Owen make an over easy egg while wearing a blindfold! (The result was a bit of a mess, but it was fun.)

Then all at once, the Chef stopped what he was doing and held up an index finger. "Smell that?"

Owen sniffed the air. "The roast?"

The Chef nodded. "Time to take it out."

He pulled out the roasting pan and tested it with a temperature probe. "Good," he said, "right at 120°. But you can't always judge by the probe. You may be aiming for 120° internal, but have to take it out at, say, 110°, because that particular cut's so big it will keep on cooking itself after you take it out. The bigger the piece of meat, the more its temperature will carry over after you take it out of the oven. You have to stay connected to the food with your senses as it cooks. . . ."

Owen struggled to take this all in. He was learning so much about cooking that sometimes he felt his head would burst.

Running through all these lessons were two questions that kept nagging at him. The first was, How do you make a dish like this for *a hundred people* and have each serving come out just right? He didn't ask; he figured he'd find out when the time came. But that brought him to the second question, which he did ask, more than once, starting with their first lesson:

"When we're actually there, at the banquet, what do you want *me* to do?"

And every time he did, the Chef waved the question away. "We'll figure something out," he'd say. Or, "You'll be part of the team, Owen, part of the team."

There were other questions playing in the back of his mind, too. Owen was only fourteen, but he wasn't naïve. It was clear to him that no matter what the Chef said, he wasn't there to "help develop the menu." (Like the Chef needed *his* help.) And even as they worked their way through dish after dish, Owen couldn't help thinking that the Chef already knew exactly what he wanted for that banquet menu.

So why was he there? It felt like he was cramming a few years of culinary school into four or five weeks. Maybe that was it. Maybe the Chef just wanted him to be trained up and ready to serve as a fully functioning part of the team for the big day.

Which was more than he could say about his baseball coach at school, who seemed to see Owen more as a problem than an asset.

When try-outs wrapped, Owen had not made starting pitcher after all. He did make relief pitcher, barely, to which Mom said, "At least that's *something*, honey, you have to admit." Owen had to agree with that, but it did not make him feel any less disappointed.

And so the rest of April slipped away, then most of May.

༄

And then one day, Will started talking.

It was a Monday, always a slow day, and they were alone together in the kitchen prepping for a sparse dinner clientele. Maybe it was the fact that the banquet was just a week away, and no doubt Will was thinking about that, since he was (as far as Owen knew) going to play a central role there. Or maybe it was the fact that Owen had been there for long enough that he'd started feeling like family, the way Mad Dog and Bernie and Ruth did. Maybe Will was starting to get comfortable with him being around.

Or maybe it was none of those things.

Owen honestly had no idea just what it was that set this miracle in motion. But whatever it was, on this particular Monday, in the middle of the afternoon lull, as the two were washing the dirt out of a huge batch of leeks for a leek-and-potato soup they were about to make, Will spoke up.

"You been good for the Chief."

Good for him? Owen had no idea what he meant by that, or how to respond.

Will kept talking.

"I've heard him telling you about his rules. You know. *Taste everything, improve every dish, the little things are the big things.* All that." He glanced at Owen as he worked. "I ever tell you what he used to do?"

Will had hardly ever told Owen *anything*, let alone stories about the Chef, but Owen just shook his head.

"You'd be just starting to plate a dish to send it out to the front, and he'd stop you. 'Hang on there! Let's look at what we've got here. White fish, white potatoes, green vegetable. Blah. Too elementary. Boring. I like the striped bass, but not the way the potatoes and broccoli go with it. I like the elements, but not the composition. What can we do? How can we make it better? . . .'

"Meanwhile," (Will was warming to his story—Owen didn't dare breathe for fear of stopping the flow) "you're standing there, you've got customers out there who are reaching the bottom of their second martini, seconds are ticking by. . . ."

New York, thought Owen. *He's talking about New York.*

"And the Chief goes, 'Let's take off the broccoli, go with spinach and arugula sautéed with prosciutto, maybe swap out the potato for a broiled marinated tomato. Maybe add some saffron-poached pearl couscous, tossed in with the spinach. Garnish with yellow pepper coulis. And hey, let's coriander-dust the fish. Okay, okay. Good. Now it's starting to look like a thing of beauty.'"

Will chuckled.

"And meanwhile you've got three different guys all frantically whipping up everything he just described, and the plate now looks like an Indy 500 car in mid-circuit maintenance, with a pit crew of guys all frantically trying to service it and get it back out on the track in time.

"We turned it into a game. *What's Chief gonna do?* We'd be minutes away from serving a party of three hundred, and he'd walk past the entrée and say, *This could be better! Improve everything you touch!*"

Will told Owen that back in New York, the "Chief" became

known as the go-to guy to work with if you wanted over-the-top parties and wild culinary feats of derring-do. He described the outrageous ice sculptures hanging from the ceiling, massive pulled sugar centerpieces, innovative appetizers that would show up the next morning in breathless prose on the pages of the *Times*'s restaurant reviews.

"You know the nursery rhyme, Sing a Song of Sixpence? One time, I kid you not, he actually put together this huge blackberry pie, and sonofagun if when he broke it open at the table he didn't have two dozen songbirds bail out of that thing and fly around the freakin' ceiling, chirping and warbling like a Radio City Music Hall chorus line."

He laughed.

"How many of his rules he tell you about so far? He tell you about Rule Six?"

Owen shook his head and said, "Just five." He was afraid to say any more than that. If he did, maybe it would break the spell and Will would stop talking.

"Well, Rule Six . . . now, that one sounds simple. But it isn't. He used to quote Thomas Watson, if you can believe *that*, the IBM guy: 'If you want to achieve excellence, you can get there today—as of this second, quit doing less-than-excellent work.'" Will chuckled. "*That's* his Rule Six. *Commit to excellence.* Good is never enough. The only acceptable standard is *excellent.*

"To the Chief, it boiled down to two words: *no compromise.* The man had no tolerance for mediocrity, and no tolerance for compromise. No tolerance at all."

Will paused, lost in thought. Owen decided to risk another two whole words.

"Sounds tough."

Sure enough, it seemed to get Will going again.

"Oh, he was tough on us, all right. He was tough on everyone. Toughest on himself, though. He came in earlier than anyone else, left later than everyone else, worked harder, pushed harder."

And then Will's voice changed completely: it got lower and rougher, the words more bitten off and dry. With a start, Owen realized he was doing a pitch-perfect Chef Kellaway impression.

"*"Commit to excellence" means never sacrificing quality, for any reason. Ever. And that takes a commitment, because quality almost always takes longer, costs more, and is more difficult. But the question "Is it worth it?" never occurs to you. It's like breathing. You never stop to wonder if all that exhaling and inhaling is really worth the effort. Know why? 'Cause you're already committed.'*"

Will took a big breath, like it had taken a massive effort to stay in character that long, and then he laughed again, and this time Owen laughed, too. He really did do an excellent Chef.

"Haven't heard him talk about these things for years. Not since way before he retired. I think the last time he—"

"Hang on." Owen completely forgot his reluctance to talk. "*Retired*? What do you mean?"

Will picked up his knife again. Owen sensed that the recitation was drawing to a close.

"He doesn't need to come in here, man. He's got Mad Dog and me and the rest. He's retired. He just comes in out of habit—that, and to make sure we aren't messing everything up.

"Though I have to say," he added, as he turned back to his station and started prepping the potatoes, "since you've been here, he's been coming in a helluva lot more." And he concluded by coming back to the thought he'd started with:

"You been good for him."

Which Owen didn't get any more now than he did the first

time Will said it. *Good for him*? How?

As he joined in on the potatoes, he thought about Rule Six. *Commit to excellence.* Was he "excellent"? He certainly was trying hard, and he'd done an awful lot of cooking in the past few months. The Chef hadn't ever said he was disappointed in Owen's efforts, not in so many words. He'd even said things like, "Good, Owen," or "Good work," more than once.

Still, he hadn't yet served one of Owen's Chef Specials, not to a single customer.

12

complications

That night Owen was in his room doing his homework when he heard the phone ring. He heard his mom talking softly in the next room, but he tuned it out. He didn't even realize she was still on the phone when, about five minutes later, there came a knock on his door.

He opened to find his mom holding the phone out to him.

"It's Ruth," she said. "From the diner. Bernie had the baby." Her face was pale, and Owen's heart lurched in his chest. Something was wrong.

"Ruth?" he said into the phone. "How is she, is she okay? Is the baby okay? Is everything all right?"

Ruth's reply was cautious. "Not . . . entirely. It's way ahead of schedule, Owen. She wasn't due for seven weeks yet."

Bernie had had a rough time with the delivery, Ruth explained. There were complications. She was going to be in the hospital for at least three or four days, maybe longer.

"And the baby?" asked Owen.

Ruth's voice paused, ever so briefly. "Honestly, honey, it's touch

and go with the baby. I'll let you know the moment I hear anything, okay?" she said.

Owen didn't know what to say.

That night it took him forever to get to sleep.

Owen knew something, a thing nobody on earth knew that
he knew.

One Saturday morning, just the summer before, he awoke to
hear his mom crying softly in the next room. Alarmed, he crept
downstairs and found his father in the kitchen, staring out the
kitchen window, the untouched pancake ingredients spread out
on the island counter behind him. He turned with a start when he
heard Owen enter, and immediately his face relaxed.

"C'mere, buddy," he said, patting the empty stool. Reading the
question on his son's face, he took another stool himself and sat
next to him. "Your mom'll be okay. She's just . . . she's feeling kinda
blue today."

Owen knew there was something happening here beyond *feeling kinda blue.* "What's wrong?" he said.

His father hesitated, then looked at Owen. And then he told
him.

Years ago, when Owen was not quite two years old, they'd had
another child, a little girl. "Your sister," he said. But there had been
complications, and the baby had died in childbirth. "It was a rough
time for a while there. Those were hard years. You were too little to
know what was going on, which was a blessing, in more ways than
one. And of course, you kept your mother mighty busy, too, growing like a weed," he added with a huge smile, "and that was such a
gift for her, you can't imagine. For both of us. Still, sometimes the
old hurt rears its head."

He was silent for a moment.

"Like today?" said Owen.

His father nodded. "Like today."

A thought came into Owen's head, and the moment it did he knew it was true. "It's today, isn't it. Today's her birthday. My sister's birthday."

His father looked at him, surprised, then gave a thoughtful smile and nodded slowly. "You've grown into a wise young man, Owen."

Owen lay on his bed, thinking back to that day and hearing his father's voice. *You've grown into a wise young man, Owen.* He wondered what his father would think of him now. He wished he could talk to his mother about it all—the sister he never knew, that "rough time" all those years ago. He had almost brought it up, more than once. But didn't she already have enough sadness to deal with, right here and now?

৵

All through school the next day, the only thing Owen could think about was Bernie and her "little man." He hoped they were both all right. He hoped the little guy had ten fingers and ten toes.

The moment school let out, Owen raced to the diner, hoping to hear that everything was okay now. He found Ruth alone at the counter, and one look at her face told him: so far, nothing had changed. Things at the hospital hadn't gotten worse, Ruth said, but they hadn't gotten significantly better, either. There was nothing to do but wait.

It was a cool, windy day out, and Owen's nose and ears were red from the ride over. Ruth could see how upset he was. "Hang on," she said. She whipped him up a cup of her special hot choco-

late laced with ancho chili, vanilla bean, and sea salt—his favorite—then went to the far end of the counter to serve a customer.
After a moment she came back and stood by Owen, gazing out at
the windy day, offering wordless comfort.

After a long minute, Owen spoke up, his voice thick with
emotion. "Why are there always . . . *complications?*"

Ruth was quiet for a moment. Then she said, "Here's how I see
it. Some things are good, and true, and never change. Not many,
but a few. And everything else? . . . like leaves in the wind. Blow
any which way, and you can't control it."

Put your effort into controlling the sail, Owen thought, *not the
wind.*

He took a long sip of his spicy hot chocolate and looked up at
Ruth. "Yeah? So what's good and true and never changes? What
are those few things?"

Ruth gave her faint smile and said, "Well, Owen. That's what
we're all here to find out, isn't it."

The next day, Wednesday, Owen desperately wanted to race to the
diner after school again—but he couldn't. He had been handed an
unexpected obligation.

This coming Saturday, his team had a big game. The biggest
game of the season, in fact, playing a nearby school that was their
arch-rival. And on Tuesday afternoon, while Owen had been sitting on his diner stool sipping on his hot chili chocolate and talking with Ruth, their starting pitcher had gotten in a fight with
another boy and hurt his hand. Hurt it too bad to pitch. Which
meant Owen would now be pitching in the starting lineup, after
all.

Under any normal circumstance this would have been great

news, the best of news, but it also meant that, as a key player in the big game, he would now be critical to their practice sessions after school every afternoon for the rest of the week—just as everyone else at the diner would be gearing up for the banquet. Just when his team (his *other* team, that was) needed him most!

Another complication.

Even in the midst of practice that day, Owen kept wishing he could be in town at the diner, waiting with the others.

The same thing happened the next day, too, the after-school practice (which should have been exciting) dragging heavily on until dark.

That evening, Thursday, Owen went with the Chef to visit the auditorium where the big event would be happening the following Monday to do a walk-through of the kitchen.

Owen had never seen anything so massive. There were rows and rows of stainless steel racks on wheels, an endless line of burners and convection ovens, a walk-in the size of Owen's living room, and a charbroiling station the size of Texas, where the banquet's entrées would be sizzling just four days from now.

The menu had long been established by now. It would include a chicken consommé with Parisienne vegetables (carved into perfect little spheres, like mini–melon balls), a frisée salad, and a charbroiled filet of beef tenderloin with oyster mushrooms perched on a bed of potato/parsnip/chive purée and assorted vegetables.

"You know every one of these dishes inside and out, Owen," said the Chef. "You know the feel of them, the smell, the taste. You know the extra steps it takes to make each one come together beautifully—as a single dish."

He looked around the massive galley, a general surveying the field on the eve of battle.

"Monday, we do it for a crowd.

"Monday, we go from putting together a single perfect plate to doing the same thing, precisely and economically, with the same exquisite care and passion—only for an auditorium full of people."

He turned and looked at Owen. "The challenge is to keep all the details of real food—real seasoning, real timing, cooked just to perfection, no more, no less—and to do it with the precision of an auto plant assembly line."

He looked around the place again.

"It's all in how you compose the space, Owen. *Mise en place* on a massive scale."

Owen didn't say a word. He was itching to ask the same old question again—"What will you be expecting *me* to do?"—but he knew that if he did, the Chef would just say, "We'll see."

There had been no news yet about Bernie or the baby.

At eight o'clock the next morning, while Mad Dog cooked for the Friday morning rush, Will met the Chef at the diner's little loading dock to take delivery on some of the items they'd be prepping over that weekend.

There were cases of potatoes and parsnips, broccolini and cipollini, summer squash and butternut squash, oyster mushrooms and black trumpet mushrooms, apples and pears and pecans. There were flats of garlic and shallots and chives, rosemary, thyme, and chervil. Olive oil and truffle oil, champagne vinegar and white balsamic vinegar. Cases of whole chickens, cases of beef tenderloin, cases of bacon—and of course, bags and bags of onions, carrots, and celery.

Everything was tallied and checked against the lists the Chef had compiled, then double-checked and finally hauled inside and set aside to await the countdown that would begin Sunday morning.

They did not hear from Owen all that day.

Not a word.

The Chef hoped his practice was going well, and that the pressure of the big game the next day, layered onto the stress of worrying about Bernie and her baby, would not be too much for him. So did Will and Ruth.

All that day at work, Owen's mom worried about Bernie and her baby, too, but even more so about Owen, wondering how her son was managing his day, both at school and at practice, thinking about the ache in his eyes, wishing she could do more to protect him and make his sadness go away.

All around Mapletown that Friday, thoughts were tuned to Owen, wishing him well, hoping he was doing okay, fearing that he wasn't.

⬦

Saturday morning at oh eight hundred, the phone in the Chef's home office rang. He picked it up after the first ring.

"Hi, Chef? It's Owen."

"I know, Owen. I recognized the voice."

"Oh. Right." Silence.

"What's up, Owen?" said the Chef.

"I was wondering if you need me today. I mean, if there's anything I can do."

The next five or six seconds ticked by silently. The Chef knew that whatever had happened that had Owen on the phone offering his services for the day instead of getting ready for the big game, it couldn't be good.

"Don't you need to be at the ballpark today, Owen?" he said gently.

"Nah," said Owen. "I was supposed to, but . . ." He paused. "There were complications."

The Chef decided not to push it. "That's fine, Owen," he said. "Why don't you come by my house later, say, in two hours? I'm making a little extra chicken stock, for blanching the Parisienne. You can help dice and sauté the mirepoix."

When Owen showed up at the Chef's door two hours later, all the concealer his mom had applied that morning could not conceal the fact that he had been in another fight. Maybe his worst yet.

If the Chef noticed, he gave no indication. Of course, thought Owen, he *must* have noticed. But the Chef didn't say a word, which in a way made him feel even worse. Relieved as he was not to have to explain, there was a part of him that wanted to confess, to tell the whole story, that wanted the Chef to *know* what had happened.

They had broken into two teams during Friday afternoon practice for a mock game. The "game" had not gone well. Owen was so distracted he was pitching terribly, and by the fourth inning he was embarrassed and steaming mad. Mad enough to get in a fist fight with a kid from the "opposing team," which resulted in his being not only yanked off the mound but also suspended—*for the rest of the season.*

Build your team? Ha. Owen had *ruined* his team. So much for Rule Five. And Rule Six, too. And every other rule, for that matter.

His father would be so disappointed in him.

The Chef did not ask what had happened, or ask anything at

all. He set Owen up at the island, and Owen went to work on his mirepoix.

He peeled a bowl of onions, peeled his carrots, washed and trimmed his celery, then reduced all his vegetables to uniform, geometrically squared-off planks of miniature edible lumber. Then, time to dice. He was by this time well practiced at the process, and did a decent job of it.

Now, to cook.

He set a large sauté pan over a burner, added some butter to the pan to melt, then added his onions, then the rest. . . .

That idiot. Owen was thinking about the kid he'd fought with during practice the day before. *He'd probably laugh at me if he saw me doing this. But I'll bet he couldn't pull this dish off to save his life. . . .*

After a minute or so his attention returned to the pan—and the moment it did he yanked it off the burner. It was too late.

He'd burned the mirepoix.

Owen's face went red. "*Stupid!*" he muttered. He scraped the pan's contents into the trash and started over: peeling the onions, peeling the carrots, washing and trimming the celery. . . .

The Chef didn't say a word.

The onions had made Owen's eyes burn this time, and his vision was a little blurry. He wiped them furiously with his sleeve. He would not cry.

He finished his dice and looked it over. Once again, a very decent job. He took a deep breath, then got it going in the pan.

He couldn't believe he had let that first batch burn. He didn't know which made him madder: that he'd messed up, or that the Chef had seen him do it. Actually, that was an easy question: neither one. What made him maddest was that he'd been booted off the team because of that stupid fight. Which was *so* not fair, because it wasn't even his fault: that obnoxious kid had been taunting him right from the first inning—

Suddenly the Chef was whisking his pan off the burner and setting it off to the side on a trivet.

"What are you—?" Owen stopped midsentence and looked with horror at the pan.

He'd burned this one too. *Stupid, stupid, stupid!* he thought. He was afraid to look up and meet the Chef's eyes.

When he did, the Chef was looking at him as calmly as ever, with no expression. "Owen," he said, "would you be able to come back over here for a while, first thing tomorrow morning?"

The next day was Sunday, the day before the banquet. The team would already be heavily into prep, most of which would take place at the diner, which, for the first time in many years, would be closed to business for the day.

"Tomorrow?" Owen stammered. "But I thought . . . aren't we all prepping at the diner tomorrow?"

"You can join the others in the afternoon," the Chef said quietly. "I have some work for you here in the morning, if that's okay."

Owen sighed. "Sure, I guess."

"Good," said the Chef, as he began cleaning up the kitchen and putting things away. "Say, oh nine hundred?"

Owen stared at him. "Wait," he said. "You mean—you're sending me *home*? But I just got here!"

The Chef continued putting things away as he spoke. "A man I very much respect once told me, 'Here's the thing to know about holes. When you find yourself in one, stop digging.'"

He stopped for a moment and looked at the boy, then spoke softly. "Come back tomorrow, Owen."

❧

That night the phone rang again at Owen's home, and once again he heard his mom talking quietly in the next room—only this time Owen tried as hard as he could to overhear what was being said. And this time it was less than a minute before the knock came on his door.

His mom held out the phone with a single word, "Ruth," and from her tone and the look on her face Owen instantly knew things were going to be all right.

"Ruth?" he said into the phone. "Is she okay?"

She was. Bernie was out of the ICU and doing well. Her little boy was going to be okay, too. He did in fact have ten fingers and ten toes, and he could both see and hear just fine. His mom had named him Thomas.

Thomas.

What was it Ruth had said, that first Saturday? When he'd come in for his big "test" and tried to show off by making two over easy eggs?

A lot of people knew your father.

13

honor

Sunday morning at nine o'clock sharp, Owen stood at the Chef's front door. Mrs. Kellaway greeted him warmly and took him back to the kitchen, where the Chef was sitting on a tall stool, drinking hot tea and poring over a copy of some international chefs magazine.

"Ah," said the Chef. He set down his tea and magazine and led the boy back through a small hallway into what seemed to Owen like a large mudroom, bristling with shovels and spades and rakes and trowels.

"Grab some gloves," he said, "and follow me." He took a hoe and a basket of seeds and led Owen out into the backyard, where Mrs. Kellaway's massive garden spread out before them like a miniature city, its streets and alleyways punctuated by birdfeeders, large flowering plants, and other distinctive landmarks.

"You ever done this before?" the Chef inquired.

Owen wasn't sure exactly what "this" was. He shook his head.

"Don those gloves, son," the Chef said. "We've got some planting to do."

"We" turned out to mean *Owen*. After showing him how to hoe a row, then fertilize it, plant some seeds, fertilize again, and water, the Chef left Owen with his packets of seeds and garden tools. "Have to go check on the prep." And he drove off to the diner, where the others were no doubt already busy at work.

Alone in the garden, Owen looked at the seeds. There were green beans, kale, three kinds of lettuce, beets, onions, shallots, and carrots. Lots and lots of carrots. Owen couldn't believe how tiny those seeds were. *One good sneeze*, he thought, *and I'd blow them all away.*

It took him a solid three hours under the hot sun to get all the seeds in, and the whole time he seethed with frustration. Everyone else was over at the diner prepping for the banquet. The thing was happening tomorrow night! And the Chef had him out here digging in the dirt? Was he crazy?

The Chef reappeared just as Owen was finishing the last row of carrots.

"C'mon inside for a bite," he said. "You must be hungry."

You must be hungry? Furious, was more like it. Owen felt like hurling his trowel through the kitchen window. But he said nothing, just trudged inside, put his garden tools down in the mud room, and went into the kitchen to wash his hands.

The Chef had prepared some bruschetta with homemade mozzarella, shaved Parmesan, fresh basil (from the garden, of course), and a drizzle of thick, reduced balsamic. It was exquisitely delicious, but even that yummy crunchy gooey savory-sweet-tart amazingness could not dissipate the dark clouds over Owen's mood.

While they ate, the Chef walked Owen through how he made the dish. Owen hardly heard a word. His taste buds automatically registered the explosions of flavor, but his mind was approximately fifty yards away, still fuming about being stuck out in that garden for hours.

After the Chef finished his explanation, they ate in silence. The Chef finished a few bites ahead of Owen, pushed back his plate, and spoke up again.

"So, Owen. Those carrot seeds you just planted? They'll be ready to harvest in twelve weeks or so. Toward the end of the summer, Mrs. Kellaway and I will go out, pull those carrots, bring them in the house, clean and wash them, and cook them."

Owen nodded, as he finished his last bite.

The Chef looked at him. "You know what I'm saying?"

Owen stopped chewing. "Um . . . not really."

"It'll take twelve weeks to regrow what you burned and threw in the trash yesterday."

Owen looked down at his hands. He didn't know what to say.

"Someone," the Chef continued, "went out onto a field and got the soil ready, bending over till their backs were sore getting the fertilizer just right, put the seeds in the ground, tended to the weeds, and eventually went back out, pulled and busheled those carrots. It took months of time and effort to put them into your hands, for you to burn them and toss them in the trash without a thought."

"I understand," Owen mumbled, his cheeks burning red.

"I'm not sure you do. I'm not scolding you, Owen, or saying this to make you feel bad. Honest mistake in the kitchen? Happens all the time. Part of the process. But that, yesterday? That wasn't an honest mistake. You were careless. You were going through the motions but not focusing on those carrots and onions at all. You weren't *with* them, you were off somewhere else.

"What I'm saying, Owen, is never forget that those are chunks of life in your hands. Never forget where they came from."

He paused. When Owen said nothing, he continued.

"Those last three hours? That wasn't punishment. That was perspective. When you put those seeds in the ground yourself, it gives you a whole different understanding. You treat your carrots with respect, because you know where they came from. You find yourself making damn sure you use what you have to the absolute best of your abilities."

Owen was silent.

"Okay," said the Chef, "now help me put this stuff away."

As the Chef moved the bruschetta pan from stove to sink, Owen went for the big bowl of mozzarella soaking in cold water on the counter, to put it in the fridge. He grabbed the bowl, swiveled—and the moment he did, the thought flashed through his mind that he had not bothered to wash his hands, which were still a little greasy from the bruschetta. But the thought came too late. His grip on the smooth stainless steel slid away, and the entire bowl and its contents went crashing to the floor.

"*Crap!*" he shouted. "I can't *believe* I did that!"

The Chef spoke evenly. "Don't worry about it, Owen, it's—"

"I'm so sorry! *I'm so sorry*! I can't *believe* I was so *stupid*!"

"Owen." His voice firm but quiet. "It's nothing. Don't—"

But Owen was a runaway train of emotions, and nothing was going to stop or even slow his headlong plunge off the tracks.

"Why was that *stupid* thing so *slippery*, anyway! Why did that *stupid bowl* have to be so *heavy*! Why are we even *making* all this *stupid food*!! *THIS WHOLE THING IS STUPID*!!!"

Owen glared at the Chef—and then, to his horror, he did that very thing he had worked so hard, for so many weeks, so many months, not to do.

He burst into tears.

The Chef covered the ground between them in two strides

and encircled the boy in his arms, containing him in a bear hug, saying nothing, while Owen sobbed and sobbed and sobbed his heart out.

The Chef held him for a full minute, not moving, not saying a word.

Then he said softly, "Owen. Is it okay if I say something about your father?"

Owen was still sobbing, his face buried in the Chef's chest, but he managed a nod.

The Chef took a breath, then let it out. "I knew him, you know. I knew your father."

Owen's sobs were quieter; he nodded again.

"Owen, your father's death makes absolutely no sense. All those things people have probably told you—*he's in a better place, God has a plan, time will heal your pain*—those people mean well, but I know that all that does nothing for you whatsoever. And I can't offer any better. Honestly, I have no idea why he's gone or what it all means.

"All I know is, your father was a great man. And he loved you more than anything else on this earth."

His sobs growing still quieter, Owen nodded again into the Chef's chest.

"I know this, too," the Chef continued. "Searching for where to put the blame just keeps the hurt alive in the worst way. And it's a colossal waste of the most precious thing you have. Which is every moment of your amazing life."

Owen pulled back now, just enough so he could look up at the Chef.

"You can keep looking for someone or something to blame," the Chef said, "but that's a hunt that will go on forever. There is no one to blame." He released his hug. And just when Owen thought there was nothing the man could do or say that could surprise him anymore, the Chef said this:

"So, Owen, here's the question you have to ask yourself: Are you going to waste your life getting even with the world—or are you going to get up off your butt and make something out of yourself?"

For a tense moment Owen glared at him.

Then the Chef said, "Tell you what, don't answer right away. You can get back to me on that. Right now let's finish up here and get over to the diner. Okay?"

Owen felt such a jumble of emotions, he hardly trusted himself to speak. Hearing the Chef talk about his father made him feel the grief all over again, but in a strange way it was also a huge relief—he'd been aching to have this conversation for weeks. But . . . was it really over already? Was that all they were going to say? What about his father and the Chef—how did they know each other?

But he was already in motion, his training kicking in. *Clean as you go.*

The Chef washed out the pan and utensils in the sink. Owen picked up the spilled mozzarella, got out the mop, and cleaned the floor. Neither spoke.

Until, when they were nearly finished, the Chef commented, "By the way, Louise and I both saw what you did out there." Nodding in the direction of the garden. "Good work, Owen, really good work. Excellent."

Excellent.

Owen was so startled he nearly tipped over the mop bucket. He didn't think he'd ever heard the Chef speak that word to him, and certainly not in reference to anything Owen himself had done.

Excellent.

The Chef was drying and putting away a spatula. If he had any clue the effect his words had had on Owen, he didn't show it.

Owen stared at him. Then he said, "Chef? About what you said, before?"

The Chef turned, put the spatula down, and gave Owen his full attention.

"I do," said Owen. "I do want to get up off my butt and do something with my life."

The Chef looked at Owen for a brief eternity, and then did something that Owen had never, ever, seen him do before.

He smiled.

Owen thought it was possibly the faintest smile he'd ever seen, and it didn't last for more than a few seconds, but it was a real, actual *smile*, all right. It looked so out of place on the Chef's face, Owen almost laughed.

And then the Chef said, "Good. Because I need you to cook the entrée for the banquet tomorrow night."

It took Owen five or six seconds to fully register what he'd just said. "Wait—WHAT? *Me*? Are you kidding me? For *a hundred people*?"

"Not a hundred, Owen. Three hundred."

"*WHAT*? But . . . I thought *you* were going to cook the entrée! That's the most critical piece of the whole thing! You told me so!"

The Chef shrugged. "I can't, Owen. I'm going to be out front, up on stage. I'm part of the event."

Owen's mind staggered, trying to wrap itself around the magnitude of cooking perfect filets for not one, not two, not ten, but *three hundred people*.

"Wait!" he said. "Why can't Will do it?"

The Chef shrugged again. "Will's part of it, too. He'll be up there with me."

"What about Mad Dog? Mad Dog would help—he's the *best*, he could *totally* do it!"

The Chef nodded. "Mad Dog will be there, yes, and he'll be in charge of the whole operation. But I need *you* to be in charge of the entrée."

"But . . . why didn't you give me more notice?!" stammered Owen. "If I'd had a week, I could have practiced more! I could have been more prepared!"

"Owen," said the Chef. "You're as prepared as you could possibly be. If you'd had a week, you'd have spent it getting nervous. You'd probably be on a bus by now, heading for the Canadian border."

"But I could blow this whole thing! Why are you putting this on me? Why would you trust me not to totally screw this up?"

The Chef didn't answer right away. He sat pursing his lips and frowned—like he was thinking something over. After a moment, he looked at Owen and said, "Hang on."

He got up and left the kitchen. A minute later he came back in carrying a polished wooden box the size of a small briefcase.

"The thing is," he said, "your father and I? We were business partners."

Business partners. Owen shook his head, too dumbfounded to speak. Finally. They were going to have the conversation—the *whole* conversation. He was going to learn about the Chef and his father.

"I used to run a restaurant in New York. A very nice restaurant. Great reviews, top Zagat ratings, the whole thing."

Owen nodded. *Will told me*, he thought, but he kept silent.

"Your father and I, we knew each other from the army. He worked for me there at the restaurant. Years. He was such a talent. Amazing. We made a great team."

For a moment Owen thought the tears would come rushing back, but it didn't happen. Maybe he was all sobbed out.

"Eventually he'd had enough of life in the big city, said it wasn't where he wanted to raise a family. So he moved back here with your mom." He looked at Owen. "That was when you came along.

"I have to admit, I was angry with him for leaving. Thought he was crazy, too. But it wasn't long before I realized I'd gotten tired of the big city, too. A year later, I joined him. He'd told me about this great old brownstone on a corner in the middle of town that was empty and run down, said we could pick it up for a song. So I moved here to Mapletown to go in on it with him, renovate the place, turn it into a diner."

Owen finally found his voice. "Ruth and Will came with you."

The Chef raised his eyebrows in surprise. "Ah. Of course, Ruth, our bartender." The Chef chuckled, and Owen laughed a little, too. (It was only later that he would reflect back on this conversation and notice what a miracle it was to hear an actual *chuckle* from the Chef. Right now he was too spellbound by the Chef's story to notice.)

"Your father was the one, you know, who hired Bernie. Gave her a job when no one else in town would. She says it changed her life. He changed a lot of people's lives." He paused.

Owen flashed back on the conversation he'd had with Bernie that spring day, when she'd told him about the kind man who took a chance on her, and what he'd told her. He remembered thinking it sounded like something his father would've said. No wonder. It *was* something his father said.

"The diner took an enormous amount of work to get off the ground," said the Chef, "but we all had a good time doing it. You and your mom would come in sometimes, when it was slow. You used to spin the stools, try to get them all going at once. You were tiny then." He smiled again, a distant smile that quickly slipped away. "The pace was hectic, beyond hectic. Insane. A year after we opened, your father said he wasn't being fair to you and your mom. He needed a job with more normal hours, so he could be home at night. Have dinner with his family, see you before you went to sleep."

Owen knew there was more to it than that. That this must have been when his parents lost their second child and those "hard years" began. But he held his silence.

"I got angry with him, once again," the Chef continued, "told him he was making a big mistake. I'm not proud of that."

He paused again, as if he were finding it hard to choose the right words.

"Sometimes, Owen, even best friends fight. Well, you already know that. In any case, we didn't speak after that. I should have . . ." All at once the Chef looked so sad that for one terrifying moment, Owen thought maybe *he* was going to cry. But he just shook his head once, slowly. "Mrs. Kellaway told me I was being stubborn. As usual, she was right."

Owen could see it all. His parents, grief-stricken over the loss of their infant daughter, withdrawing into themselves. The Chef, guilty over the stress that had pushed his friend so hard, angry at losing his partner. The arguments and falling-out gradually turning to stalemate and silence, like the heat of summer draining away into a winter freeze . . . and everyone who knew them tip-toeing around the situation for years afterward. Much as his teachers at school had been tip-toeing around him ever since September.

"Clean as you go," Owen said softly.

The Chef looked up from his thoughts. "Mm?"

"Always clean as you go," said Owen. "If it sits, it dries. And it's a bitch to clean later."

The Chef looked at Owen for a long moment. Then he nodded. "That it is."

Owen said, "Why didn't you say something about this before?"

The Chef hesitated. "Your life was already so complicated. I wanted to give you time to do all this—" he waved one arm around the kitchen, "on your own terms, without being caught up in events long past."

He hesitated again, then added, "I suppose I was afraid you'd be angry at me. Maybe, quit this."

He looked at Owen, gave another faint smile, and said, "In any case, here we are. And I have something for you. Not a rock, this time."

He pulled out the wooden box he'd brought out and set it on the counter. He opened it. Inside was a matching set of five beautiful carbon steel knives of different sizes, all heavily stained but gleaming and clearly sharp as razors. Owen recognized one. It was the knife he'd been using for the past four months at the diner—the one the Chef had handed him that very first day, when he learned how to dice carrots.

"These were your father's knives. I gave them to him many years ago, in New York. He always kept them in the kitchen. When he sold me his half of the diner, he left these behind. I've cleaned them up and sharpened them. They belong to you."

Inside the felt-lined top, laminated and glued into the upper left-hand corner, was a fading snapshot of Owen as a toddler with his mom. Owen dimly remembered the day that snapshot had been taken, and knew who'd been standing behind the camera.

Tears stung his eyes once more—and this time he didn't bother to wipe them off on his sleeve, and let them fall.

"You have a talent, Owen. But that wasn't your doing, that was a gift from your father. Your job is to make a difference with that gift. Don't be lazy or careless with it. Don't sit on the sidelines and let yourself be defeated by what goes wrong or what looks hard. It's human nature to be lazy and take the path of least resistance. It's like the force of gravity, always there, pulling you down. It takes a very special force to counter that gravity, and if you want to do something great with your life, you have to harness that force."

Excellence? thought Owen. *Commitment?*

"That force is *honor*," said the Chef. "If you want to counteract that gravity, you have to treat every food, every ingredient, every utensil, every customer, every colleague, with respect. Never forget where your carrots and onions came from. And never forget who you're serving.

"Your father was a man of honor, Owen. Me, I forgot my own Rule Seven.

"He never did."

Still staring at the knives, Owen turned the words over in his mind. He picked up one knife and held it close, tracing the pattern of stain on the blade and thinking about the story it told and the chef who belonged to it.

He looked up at the Chef. "That's Rule Seven. *Cook with honor.*"

More a statement than a question.

The Chef looked at the boy, then nodded. "That it is, Owen, that it is. Cook with honor. Always."

14

memorial day

At oh seven hundred Monday morning, a large van rolled up to the loading bay behind the big auditorium kitchen. Ruth and seven other people climbed out: the Chef's recon team. They moved in like a column of worker bees, buzzing through the place with practiced perfection.

The facility had already been cleaned and set up by the outfit that ran the place—but Ruth knew that no other crew cleaned to the Chef's standards. Over the next five hours they cleaned everything, from mopping the enormous floor to shining the stemware to polishing the silverware, every glass held up to the light, every place setting set with geometric precision.

Meanwhile a flurry of prep was taking place in the vast auditorium kitchen.

The broccolini was blanched in huge kettles of heavily salted water, cooked till about two-thirds done, then pulled and shocked in ice water to stop the cooking process, drained, dried, and loaded with a little butter, salt, and pepper into ten eight-by-eighteen-inch hotel pans: fire ready. All it needed was a four-minute blast in the steamer and it would be ready to serve.

The salads were assembled onto individual plates like works of art, placed on waiter trays, slid onto racks, swathed in plastic wrap, and stashed away in the huge walk-in: frisée with slices of apple and pear. Bacon for the salad was set to sauté till crispy; it would be crumbled over the plates at the last minute along with the goat cheese (which had been sliced and frozen on Sunday) before the candied pecans and white balsamic champagne vinegar dressing were added.

Owen got to witness the Chef's banquet-serve trick for mashed potatoes. They spread the potato-parsnip mix out on the bench onto plastic wrap, enough for ten portions, and rolled it up like a loaf of French bread, what the Chef called a *mashed potato cartridge*. ("Our delicious artillery.") Owen watched the team prepare thirty potato-parsnip cartridges and set them in a tall metal warmer called a "hot box." When it came time to serve, they would snip a hole in the end of a cartridge, load it into a pastry piping bag, pipe equal portions onto ten plates, remove and discard the empty plastic wrap, then slip in another hot cartridge. Nothing to clean up. Efficient. Effective.

Owen smiled as he remembered what the Chef had said about where he learned the art of *mise en place*. "In the army," he'd said. "Only they didn't call it that. They called it, *being in the army*."

Late that day, at the appointed hour, Mad Dog nodded at the stacked cases of tenderloin that Owen had pulled from the fridge an hour earlier so they could come up to room temperature. "Your territory, boss," he grinned.

Show time.

"Don't season the meat until you're ready to cook it," the Chef had warned him. "If you salt it too early and let it sit, it'll suck out the moisture, and then no attempt to sear will save it."

No boiled barn owl happening today, thought Owen.

He cracked open the cases of individually cut filets, each one trimmed to six ounces. He counted out twenty-five and tossed them in a large stainless steel bowl with fresh cracked pepper and salt and a little olive oil, then laid them out on the sizzling hot charbroiler, one at a time, moving rapidly but methodically. He knew that if he put out any more than twenty-five, the first one would be burning by the time he'd placed the last. Twenty-five was just right.

The moment he reached filet No. 25, he went back and moved the first one, rotating it horizontally ninety degrees to create a second set of grill marks exactly perpendicular to the first, then continued doing the same with the others. When he reached the last filet, he paused about a minute, then began at the first filet again, now flipping it over and repeating the process, charbroiling the steaks on the other side. When he'd gotten perfect grill marks seared into all twenty-five filets, he lifted them all onto a sheet pan and slid it onto a speed rack. At that point the tenderloins were still very rare inside, practically raw—but all perfectly seared on the outside.

He then repeated the sequence eleven more times, sliding eleven more sheet pans onto his speed rack, for a total of twelve times twenty-five: three hundred filets, ready to rock. Now they could rest until it was their turn to take center stage. All he had to do was slip those twelve sheet pans into the oven and blast them with 400-degree heat for thirteen minutes exactly, and they'd be ready to plate—each one perfect.

Now he paused: a spectacle was about to take place, and Owen planned to watch it happen. It was time for banquet service to begin, starting with the soup.

The array of three hundred individual servings looked like an installation of expensive and elaborate artwork. For hours on Sunday the banquet team had perched on tall stools, working away with their Parisienne scoops (what Owen would have called a small melon baller), carefully carving out perfect spheres of raw butternut squash, yellow summer squash, and zucchini, which were all then blanched till *al dente* in chicken stock. (The very stock Owen had been helping with on Saturday, when he had burned the mirepoix.)

That morning the Parisienne had been assembled into three hundred little timbales (small tin cups), two of each color per serving, to which they then added long, thin-cut strips ("chiffonade") of black trumpet mushroom, adding a dramatic noir visual element that cinched that expensive-artwork look. Now the sheet pans of timbales had been steamed to temperature and were lined up on the long stainless steel plating table, a regiment of soup-soldiers preparing to deploy.

Owen watched, fascinated.

As each pan slid by, the person at that station flipped each timbale into a small soup bowl, then added two or three plouches of chervil, and set the bowls up for service, ten to a tray. The chicken consommé itself was poured ripping hot into antiseptically-cleaned sparkling silver coffee urns, one urn placed in the center of each tray, which would allow Ruth's army of servers to set out the bowls dry and then pour each one tableside. Very classy—and very efficient.

As the trays began leaving for the front, the team began pulling and finishing the salad plates, which would be following the soup as next course. This was Owen's cue.

Time to fire the steaks.

He wheeled over the tall rack of filets and slid all twelve sheet pans into the 400-degree oven, then checked his watch. He had exactly thirteen minutes.

He ran back to the walk-in, pulled his rack of oyster mushrooms, and wheeled it over to the charbroiler. That morning, while Ruth's recon team made their assault on the front, Owen had been back in the huge kitchen prepping: the oysters were sorted and trimmed, placed in plastic bags, seasoned with rosemary, garlic, olive oil, pepper, and truffle oil, then carefully cryovacked, pushing the flavors into the delicate tissue of the mushrooms. Now it was time to bring them back to life.

He carefully cut open each bag and placed the mushrooms onto the hot surface. *Tssss!* Checked his watch. Six minutes. He began pulling the mushrooms, starting with the first ones he'd placed.

"Entrée veg to station!" he called out, then "Bordelaise to station!" and finally, as he ran his hot oysters over, he added, "First cartridge to station!"

And now he stood back and let the magic of the plating line take over.

He watched the plating assembly team move the food along, the regiment of heated plates filing rapidly down the long stainless steel plating table as the person manning each station added his or her singular element before sending it on:

—the first piped a one-inch-thick cylinder of potato-parsnip-chive purée onto the plate, from two o'clock to five o'clock, then

—the next added pieces of vegetable onto that purée in a random pattern, left-right-left-right: broccolini, roasted cipollini, and roasted baby carrot, then

—the next placed one filet with its beautiful char crust and charbroiled oyster mushroom topping at an artful angle onto the potato-parsnip cylinder, then

—the next added a swoosh of Bordelaise sauce to the side with a sauce gun, taking care not to sauce over the filet or mushrooms, and finally

—the finisher cleaned and wiped each plate as needed, topped it with a metal plate cover, and added it to a stack, stacking five plates high and ready for serving.

On cue, Ruth's infantry of servers began pouring through the entrance doors, loading up their trays, and charging back out the exit door.

Owen nearly fainted with relief. Production was rolling out onto the showroom floor. His mind scrambled through a replay of the last two hours, searching to see if he'd forgotten anything, missed anything, messed anything up. He couldn't find a thing wrong. Had they really pulled it off?

They had.

His work was done.

That morning, when Owen had arrived at the auditorium kitchen, the Chef took him aside and said, "Remember when I told you that you could throw a rock, or a punch, or a baseball?" Owen nodded. He still had that rock, sitting on a shelf in his room at home. "Well get ready, Chef Devon—because today, you're throwing a *party*." Once the filets were served, he'd added, Owen should exit the kitchen and come out front to be there while the event unfolded.

Now, without stopping to remove his apron, Owen slipped out

the door behind the column of servers and followed them through the corridor and in through the back of the big auditorium.

It was time to witness the party they'd thrown.

The first thing he noticed was seven men, sitting up on the stage at the other end of the hall from where he stood, all seven in uniform, some kind of military dress. The men all looked to be in their fifties except the last one in the row on the far left, who was at least a decade older than the others. It took Owen a moment to register that this last man was the Chef.

He cast his eye around the room. It was jammed with a scattered array of round tables, each one seating ten, thirty tables in all. It was only then, as he swept his view from table to table to table, that the truth of what he was seeing finally sunk in. Up until today, he had never successfully served a Chef Special to a single customer. He'd just done so now, for the first time—to *three hundred* customers.

As his eye moved back toward the stage, craning to see if he recognized anyone, he was startled to see his mother sitting at a table right out front by the stage. He'd been so focused on the operation out back for the past few hours, he had momentarily forgotten that she was going to be there, too. And she wasn't alone: she was sitting next to Louise Kellaway, the two of them talking away like old friends!

Of course, he thought. They'd known each other, hadn't they, all those years ago. They *were* old friends.

Seeing the two women together made something click for Owen. This whole thing—him learning all these lessons, becoming part of this team, putting on this banquet—all this must have been in the Chef's mind from the beginning, ever since the day

Owen had first walked into the diner looking for the owner.

But just how had that arrangement come to happen in the first place? The school had agreed not to expel him if he could work out an arrangement with the warehouse owner—but he'd never thought to wonder, who had put the school and the Chef together? Whose idea was *that?*

And the moment he posed the question, he knew the answer. A flash of memory sparked across the sky of his thoughts, an overheard phone conversation and the single word "reparation"—and he knew, with a sudden certainty, that it was Louise Kellaway his mom had been talking to that night, the night before Owen made his first visit to the diner, and that it was his mom who had placed that call.

As if she could hear his thoughts clear across the auditorium, Beth Devon suddenly looked in her son's direction and broke out in a huge smile. She beckoned him with a wave of the hand, patted the empty chair next to her, and mouthed the words, *Come sit with me.*

Just then a wave of applause broke across the room. As Owen began working his way through the maze of tables toward the front, a man stepped up to the podium and began to speak. It was Will.

"I did not originally come from Mapletown," said the uniform-clad cook, "and for this fact, you should all be grateful. As a kid, I was a freakin' mess." That brought a rustle of laughter in the audience.

"I'm not kidding. Trouble-maker in school, hellion in the neighborhood, no idea what I was doing with my life, and fully loaded with all the opinions, conviction, and rock-headed certainty of the young and clueless."

More laughter.

"Thirty-one years ago, much to my surprise, I found myself a member of the U.S. armed forces. I fought it kicking and screaming all the way. And it probably saved my life." He paused. "Although once I deployed, I very nearly *lost* my life.

"Exactly thirty years ago this week, I went through hell." He glanced at the row of men behind and to his right. "We all did. Here we were, serving in a foreign land, waist-deep in more trouble than I could ever have guessed existed anywhere on earth. I was terrified. I did not think I would get out alive. I did not think I would ever see my family, my friends, or my twenty-second birthday.

"But I did. And the only reason for that is the man sitting to my far right."

The room broke into applause again. Owen thought the Chef looked more uncomfortable than he'd ever seen him.

"Chief Warrant Officer John Kellaway was the leader of our little unit, and he took us through that hell and out the other side. He taught us how to move, how to think, how to stay safe—or at least as safe as anyone could possibly be in those circumstances. He taught us how to rise to a level we all thought impossible. We were just boys. Under his leadership, under his care, we became men.

"The Chief taught us the rules of the road, out there in the bush. Kellaway's Rules of Combat, he called them. Any one of the men on this stage could recite them perfectly, word for word, in his sleep." He looked over at the others on the stage. "Matter of fact, a few of them probably still do." This got chuckles and grins from a few of them, and from quite a few of the audience, too.

"Rule One: *Maintain Total Situational Awareness*. Never get distracted by your own thoughts; keep all your senses wide open, to everything, all the time.

"Rule Two: *Push the Envelope*. Never be content or complacent; no matter how good you think you are, you can be better. Much better. Work constantly to improve every maneuver, every drill, every skill, everything you do.

"Rule Three: *Master the Details*. No detail is so small it doesn't matter. Because how you do anything is how you do everything.

"Rule Four: *Control Your Space*. Know exactly where your weapon is, your extra ammo, your water, your knife, your compass, your chlorine tablets, your dry socks, your *everything*. You cannot control what happens to you. You can totally control how ready you are and how you respond. Have everything you need, exactly where you need it, at all times.

"Rule Five: *Build Your Unit*. The people around you are where your greatness lies. There is no solo victory. On your own, you've already lost.

"Rule Six: *Commit to Excellence*. Refuse to entertain mediocrity. Strive always to be the best and then better than that. Never compromise your standard."

He paused for a moment, looked over at the Chef, then looked out again at the crowd.

"But excellence, he taught us, is not the same thing as greatness. Excellence is just a standard. *Greatness*, he taught us, *is a choice*.

"Excellence is not greatness.

"Greatness is excellence—plus *honor*.

"That was his Seventh Rule. And Rule Seven, the Chief always told us, contained all the other rules." And here Will slipped back into that pitch-perfect Chef impression, making his voice go low and clipped. "*'If you screw up the others, just remember this one.'*" His Chief Kellaway got a warm rustle of quiet laughter throughout the room. Will smiled briefly, then grew serious again and continued in his own voice.

"Rule Seven: *Serve with honor.*

"Treat every soldier, every civilian, every weapon, every action, with respect. Respect the enemy, for that matter, even in war. And in all situations, at all times, never forget who you're serving. Who you're *honoring* with your service.

"I've never forgotten. None of us have. And there is no man on the earth whom I respect more and would rather serve than Chief Kellaway."

Will opened a small case sitting on the podium and withdrew a large medal, hanging on a lanyard of red, white, and blue ribbon. It was pure polished gold and shone like the sun. From where Owen sat he could just make out, on its face, the number "7" surrounded by a circle of letters that spelled out three words:

SERVE WITH HONOR

"Chief," said Will, "this is for you." He waited for the Chef to stand and walk over to the podium, then placed the award around his friend's neck.

Ignoring the thunder of applause, the Chef took the podium and looked around the auditorium at the three hundred gathered there. He waited for the clapping to dwindle and recede into silence.

"I'll keep this short.

"There's a man who isn't here tonight, but should be. Every one of the boys I served with was a fine soldier and an excellent human being. The finest, bravest, smartest of the lot was a kid who you all know"—and here he glanced around the auditorium—"as

Coach Devon. We knew him as Indestructible Tom. Also Thomas the Tank."

The men on stage chuckled again. Owen saw several of the men's eyes glistening with tears. So were his mom's. He squeezed her hand, and she squeezed back.

"And, later on, as Chef Thomas. Who went on to serve with me—and with Will, here—through the mortal hazards, dangers to person, and unspeakable terror known as the Manhattan fine dining scene." The audience laughed at this one, too, but it was a muted laughter, and it quickly faded back to silence as the Chef struggled to find his next words.

"Chef Thomas was the best friend I ever had.

"I miss him.

"I miss him terribly.

"It was an honor to serve with him, an honor to cook with him. An honor to know him—and his family."

He looked down at the table where Owen and his mom sat, then back at the crowd.

"In fact, that filet with oyster mushrooms you just enjoyed? That was prepared for you by his son." He looked down at their table again. "By his son, Owen Devon."

Meeting Owen's eyes, he said softly, "*Station!*"

Owen got up from his chair and climbed the steps to the stage to stand beside the Chef.

The Chef took the ribboned medal Will had given him from around his neck and put it around Owen's.

"Owen, this is for your father. Will you hang on to it for us?"

Owen felt the medal in his hand, then wrapped his arms around the Chef's middle and hugged as hard as he could, oblivious to the sounds of applause that washed through the big hall.

৵

When they got home that evening, Owen and his mom sat on stools and ate toast and talked. They talked about his dad, and about the Chef and Louise Kellaway, about New York and the early days, and about his baby sister.

That night when he drifted off to sleep he dreamt of sailing in a Sunfish with his father beside him smiling as he turned the sail and caught the wind.

15

the recipe

fourteen years later . . .

The journalist looked down at the notes he'd scribbled so far. Cordon d'Or, James Beard Foundation, Les Amis d' Escoffier Society, American Culinary Federation, Confrérie de la Chaîne des Rôtisseurs, World Association of Chefs Societies . . . the list went on and on. And of course, the big one, the grand kahuna: the Internationale Kochkunst Ausstellung—international exhibition of culinary arts. Also known as the World Culinary Olympics.

Three gold medals. And just twenty-eight years old.

The slight young man sitting across from him shifted in his seat and took a sip of tea.

But none of that was the real story, thought the journalist. Everyone already knew all those details. The journalist wanted more. What he was after, he'd told the young man on the phone when setting up the interview, was the story *behind* the story. "Our readers want to know," he'd said, "who is the man behind the starched whites? Where did he come from? What was the first step that put him on the path?"

And man, had the young chef ever delivered! He'd just heard the story behind the story, all right, all the way from the rock and the warehouse window to the banquet held in honor of old Chef Kellaway.

The young chef took another long sip of his tea, then continued.

"After that week, I never got in another fight. I pulled my grades up, graduated high school, went on to culinary school, and, well . . ."

He didn't have to finish the sentence. The journalist and everyone else in the free world knew what happened next. Chef Devon's career took a meteoric rise from there. After culinary school he went to work at an upscale resort out west and quickly rose to become Executive Chef. He had been to Germany and won his own Olympic Gold—three of them, in fact. He had made guest appearances on a handful of talk shows. Even cooked at the White House and had his own photograph of a handshake with the president.

Now, fourteen years after he began bussing tables at the Mapletown Diner to pay for a broken window, he was on the cusp of even more outrageous success. Word was, he was about to be offered his own cooking show on network television. At this very moment, even as they wrapped up the interview, he was waiting for the call that would confirm the offer.

The young chef fished in his pocket and came out with a small laminated card, the size of a playing card. "Did I show you this?" He looked at it briefly before holding it out to the journalist. "Every one of my employees carries one of these in his or her pocket at all times. I wrote it up in my notebook that same night, after my mother and I got home from the banquet. It's what I've based my career on."

The journalist took the card and read what it said:

Chef's Rules of the Kitchen

1) Taste everything.
2) Improve every dish you touch.
3) Pay attention to the little things.
4) Compose your space.
5) Build your team.
6) Commit to excellence.
7) Cook with honor.

The journalist nodded. "I love it. Kellaway's Rules of Combat become Chef's Rules of the Kitchen. '*The Ingredients of Greatness.*' Great angle."

"Turn it over," said Devon.

The journalist turned the little card over and found more type on the reverse side.

Chef's Recipe for Living

1) Savor every moment.
2) Make the world a better place with everything you do.
3) Pay attention: how you do anything is how you do everything.
4) Compose your life: put your effort into controlling the sail, not the wind.
5) Build the people around you.
6) Reject mediocrity: never compromise your standard.
7) Live with honor: treat every person with respect, and never forget who you're serving.

The journalist nodded again and said, "Mind if I keep this?" Chef Devon waved his hand, *Be my guest*, and the journalist slipped it into his pocket. "So," he continued, "do you still stay in touch, after all this time?"

Chef Devon smiled. "Let me show you something."

He pulled out his cell phone, scrolled through some photos, and held it out to the journalist. "That's my office, at home."

The photo showed the surface of a small desk and a section of wall just above it with several wall hangings. Chef Devon reached over and enlarged the one in the center. It was a small framed note, handwritten, consisting of just three lines.

> *Good job, Owen.*
> *I'm so proud of you. We all are.*
> *Your friend, John Kellaway*

"This came in the mail right after I won that post as Executive Chef," he said. "That note means more to me than any awards or medals. That's *my* Olympic gold."

The truth was, Owen and the old Chef talked on the phone every week. The Chef wrote him notes nearly every month, too, always handwritten. (Though lately he'd been threatening to finally learn how to send email, a threat that always made Owen smile.) But with Owen so busy out on the West Coast, they hadn't had the chance to actually see each other for more than a year now.

Which was something Owen was about to fix.

"Once I get word about the show, one way or the other," he told the journalist, "I'm sneaking up there to New England to surprise him and visit for a day or two before heading back west."

To pack my stuff for the move back east, he nearly added, but he knew that would have been a little presumptuous. Everyone said the show was a lock, and he did expect he'd be leaving his post out west and relocating to New York City within weeks. But still, you never knew until you knew.

He was waiting for that call.

"So what does he think about all this?" said the journalist. "Chef Kellaway, I mean."

In fact, the Chef had been over-the-moon excited for Owen and everything he'd accomplished. Owen always loved their phone calls, but this last one, especially, had really been one for the books. They'd talked on and on through the evening—about the possible TV deal, about everything Owen had learned at the resort out west, about the old days at the diner, about . . . well, about *every-thing*.

"He definitely likes the idea of my moving back east, closer to home, that's for sure." Owen smiled, thinking about how much he was looking forward to visiting with his old friend again, face to face. "He also asked me if I was sure I was ready to handle all that fame."

"And let me guess," said the journalist. "You said, yes, you were definitely ready?"

Chef Devon grinned. "I said, we'll soon find out."

His cell phone buzzed.

"Oh, wow," the journalist murmured. He could hardly believe his good fortune: he was going to be right there to witness Chef Devon's reaction to the news, good or bad. Now *that* was a good angle for his story!

But Chef Devon wasn't answering the phone. He was staring at the number. Finally, he pushed the TALK button and slowly put the phone to his ear.

"Hey," he said. For a minute he didn't say a word, just listened. Then took a big breath. "Of course," he said quietly. "I'll be there."

He disconnected the call and sat still, staring into space. Finally he looked over at the journalist.

"I'm so sorry. I have to go."

᠙

Chief Warrant Officer John Kellaway had been just weeks shy of his eightieth birthday the morning he trooped across the street to investigate. Some kid had been at the old warehouse again. *History repeats itself,* he'd sighed, as he unlocked the big side doors and slid them open. Better go see. Better go clean up the mess. Clean as you go, John, or else . . . well, you know the rest.

When he hadn't returned home by eight that evening, Louise Kellaway knew something was wrong. She called Will, who picked her up minutes later and drove her to the diner, then walked across the street with her. Will was with her when they found him.

An hour after getting the call, Owen was on the highway in a rental car, speeding north; by nightfall he was in Mapletown, pulling into the driveway of his mom's home.

That evening he cooked her blueberry pancakes and sausages, and they cried together and talked together well into the night, remembering good times they'd had, and the people they loved.

He told her about the day of his blow-up in the Chef's kitchen, how he'd dropped a bowl of mozzarella and finally burst into tears, and how the Chef had locked him in a bear hug and comforted him—and in the next breath challenged him to "get up off your butt and make something out of yourself." (This last got a good belly laugh from his mom.)

She told him how, at the age of not quite two, he had made them all laugh, running up and down the aisle in the diner, trying to get the counter stools all spinning at once. She talked about the rough time they'd gone through after losing his sister, about how she and his dad had struggled to keep their grief from casting its shadow over his buoyant little life.

He rooted around in a closet and eventually produced the rock he had saved, and told her about how the Chef had kept it for him, as the Chef had said, "to remind myself of the choices I have."

"Hang on," she said, and went upstairs. She returned a moment later toting a big leather-bound scrapbook, which she plopped down on the kitchen counter between them. She opened the cover, leafed through the first few pages, then lifted out a long stem topped by a beautiful dried blossom, brittle and perfect.

A single peach rose.

"Do you remember?" she said.

Of course he did. How could he ever forget?

That night Owen lay awake for a while in his old childhood bed, thinking about his father, and The Recipe, and about how the secret ingredient is never in the thing you're making but in who you're making it for.

The next day, on his way from the memorial service to the Kellaways' home for the reception, he thought about Bernie. She'd been at the service, of course (everyone had), and she looked terrible. He'd spent time with her, but consoling her seemed beyond anyone's ability just now.

Her boy, Thomas—her *little man*, with his ten fingers and ten toes—had fallen in with the wrong crowd. It was Thomas who'd broken into the Chef's warehouse, Thomas who made the mess the Chef was in the process of cleaning up when the stroke took him. It was hard to know who felt worse about it all: Bernie, or

Thomas himself, or . . . well, or everyone in Mapletown. But what could Owen do?

The reception was surprisingly (thankfully) upbeat, a spirited celebration of the Chef's life. Will and Mad Dog, a group of the Chef's old war buddies, a collection of colleagues and friends from New York and, it seemed, just about everyone else who'd ever been connected to the Chef in any way passed through the Kellaways' house that day. Owen had put together a simple buffet, both to feed the guests and to honor his old friend's memory in the best way he could think of. It consisted of just two dishes: platters of grilled brie and truffled crab sandwiches on brioche, meticulously trimmed and cut to finger-sandwich size; and, simmering on burners in that great open sunlit kitchen, several big kettles of chicken soup with cilantro and fresh lime.

This will heal anything you can throw at it, the Chef had said when he first made this soup for Owen. If their hearts ached the way Owen's did right now, today's guests needed all the healing they could get.

People milled about the house for a few hours. Louise and Owen had taken all the Chef's awards and commendations out of their boxes and made a display for everyone to enjoy. Owen was amazed—though not surprised—to see a number of military honors among them, including a Bronze Star with V device for Valor and a Silver Star. And, of course, his Olympic gold medals.

Toward the end of the afternoon Louise approached him quietly and said she needed to talk with him after the guests left, about the disposition of a few assets the Chef had left behind.

After they talked, Owen got in his rental car and sat, thinking about what Louise had told him.

He put his hand on his chest and closed his eyes. The sadness hurt so much he thought his heart might break apart, might shatter into a million pieces just like that big warehouse window. He had not felt an ache so acute since that year, the year he was fourteen and he'd lost his father. The year he befriended the Chef.

"He loved him, you know," his mom had said the night before as they picked at the last leftover blueberries and gazed at Beth's dried blossom, the peach rose that would shatter into a million pieces if they didn't handle it with the tenderest care. "The Chef. He loved your father like a son." She looked at Owen and added, "He loved you like a son."

Owen had just stared at her. What she was saying was perfectly true, of course; he'd just never thought about it, not in those words.

Not with *that* word.

How had Julie Landreaux put it?

"It wasn't just soup to us. It was *love*."

How had this not occurred to him before? That's what this ache was in his chest. It wasn't sadness, not really. Or it *was* sadness, of course it was . . . but underneath, it was something else entirely.

It was *love*.

He had loved that old man, loved him like a father.

He still did.

As he held that thought, the ache seemed to soften and change. It still hurt, terribly—but with a sweetness to it, along with the bitter.

Finally he opened his eyes and, once he had wiped away the tears with his hands, at least enough that he could see again, he started the car and drove.

ᠳ

They had closed the diner for the reception, but by the time Owen arrived it was open again and Ruth was there at the counter. Will in back, no doubt, prepping dinner.

Owen took off his coat and took a seat at the first stool, the one nearest the front door and pastry case. A minute later Ruth was putting a mug of hot chocolate in front of him, and one for herself, too.

"Ancho chili, vanilla bean, sea salt," she said.

He smiled, and they clinked their mugs in a wordless toast to their friend.

"Do you remember saying how you couldn't wait to get out of this town?" said Ruth.

Owen remembered.

"And you sure did, didn't you. Look at you. He was so proud of you, Owen. We all are. I know I certainly am."

Owen nodded an acknowledgment and smiled again, but his mind was elsewhere. He was still thinking about the conversation he'd just had with Louise. That, and his unshared news.

Early that morning he had finally gotten that other call, the one about the television deal. It was thumbs up. Any other time, he would have been bursting with the news, celebrating with his friends over champagne toasts.

He hadn't told anyone at all, not even his mom.

"You know he still talked about renovating that place," Ruth mused, nodding in the direction of the old warehouse. "Putting in his sinks and walk-ins and ovens and stovetops." She gave a gentle laugh. "I wouldn't be surprised if that's what he was thinking about, about exactly how he'd do it, how he'd set it up, when he was over there cleaning up that mess."

Owen stared into his mug.

"So, what are you going to do?" said Ruth. "I mean, about Thomas? It's up to you, right?"

Owen glanced at her in surprise, then smiled faintly. The diner's bartender. All these years later, and still she was always first to know things. He took another sip of his spicy hot chocolate, then nodded slowly. "That it is," he said. "That it is."

And it was, in fact, up to him. Because the "few assets" that Louise had needed to talk to Owen about included the Chef's extensive collection of menus and cooking notes, and his own set of chef's knives, which he had detailed in his will and deeded over to Owen—along with the diner itself.

And the warehouse.

My gift to you, said the brief handwritten note attached to the will. *Throw a party.*

Which meant that, as owner of the property that had been vandalized, it was now Owen's choice as to whether or not to press charges.

The kid is only fourteen, he thought.

"I know," said Ruth, reading his thoughts. "Talk about ironic, huh?"

Owen took another sip. "Sometimes I think back to that day," he said. "Picking up that rock and hurling it through that window. I still can't believe I did that."

"You were a hurting kid, Owen," she said.

They both sat for a moment, looking past the diner's empty booths, through the window and out at the old building across the street.

There it stood, dark and deserted, its four stories of weathered brickwork gazing back at them, one big window gaping like an extracted tooth.

"You know, Owen," said Ruth softly, "there are a lot of hurting kids here."

Owen nodded again. He was sure that was true.

The television show was an excellent opportunity, possibly the most excellent he'd ever seen. Golden. But, how had Will put it? *Excellence is not greatness. Greatness is excellence—plus honor.*

He thought about Bernie's boy, Thomas—her little man—and about what Bernie had said that spring day, what Owen's own father had told her when she was a young kid in trouble. *You can't wait for the world to make you happy. What makes you happy is the choices you make.*

He took a big breath, then made a decision. Let the breath out again. And smiled. *Patience*, he told himself. *A lot of great cooking is patience.* TV could wait. It wasn't going anywhere. There was a school he needed to build first.

And right now, there was a hurting boy who needed to learn how to chop onions.

chef's rules

Chef's Rules of the Kitchen

1) Taste everything.
2) Improve every dish you touch.
3) Pay attention to the little things.
4) Compose your space.
5) Build your team.
6) Commit to excellence.
7) Cook with honor.

Chef's Recipe for Living

1) Savor every moment.
2) Make the world a better place with everything you do.
3) Pay attention: how you do anything is how you do everything.
4) Compose your life: put your effort into controlling the sail, not the wind.
5) Build the people around you.
6) Reject mediocrity: never compromise your standard.
7) Live with honor: treat every person with respect, and never forget who you're serving.

owen's recipes

- ❖ Prime Tenderloin of Beef with Green Peppercorn Sauce, Cipollini Onions, and Wild Oyster Mushrooms
- ❖ Frisée Salad with Macadamia Nuts, Poached Egg, and Truffle Oil
- ❖ Chicken Soup with Cilantro and a Squeeze of Lime
- ❖ Grilled Brie and Truffle Crab Sandwich
- ❖ New England Omelet
- ❖ Chicken Stock
- ❖ Chef's "Landreaux Special" Chicken and White Bean Soup
- ❖ Chicken Consommé
- ❖ Prime Rib
- ❖ Owen's Favorite Hot Chocolate
- ❖ Bruschetta with Tomato, Fresh Mozzarella, and Fresh Basil
- ❖ Chicken Consommé with Parisienne Vegetables
- ❖ Frisée Salad with Goat Cheese, Apples, Pears, Smoked Bacon, and Candied Pecans
- ❖ Chive, Parsnip, and Potato Purée
- ❖ Charbroiled Prime Filet of Beef Tenderloin with Oyster Mushrooms and Bordelaise Sauce
- ❖ Broccolini, Roasted Cipollini, and Baby Carrots
- ❖ Chef Thomas's Famous Oat Blueberry Pancakes

To see Chef Carroll demonstrate and discuss a selection of recipes from the book, visit TheIngredientsofGreatness.com.

prime tenderloin of beef with green peppercorn sauce, cipollini onions, and oyster mushrooms

Yields: 1 serving

1 6-oz prime filet of beef tenderloin
6 small oyster mushrooms, trimmed and brushed clean of soil
3 small cipollini onions, peeled and quartered
2 tsp brined green peppercorns
1 tsp garlic, minced
1 tsp shallots, minced
1 sprig rosemary
1 sprig thyme
2 cloves garlic (whole and peeled)
¼ cup red wine
¼ cup rich veal stock (*demi-glace*, available in fine food shops)

2 Tbsp unsalted butter for filet baste
   olive oil
   kosher salt and fresh ground pepper
1 Tbsp unsalted butter to finish the sauce

Let the filet sit at room temperature for 30 minutes. Season with fresh ground pepper and kosher salt and drizzle with a teaspoon of olive oil.

Preheat sauté pan on medium heat. Pour 2 tsp of olive oil into the base of the pan, add garlic cloves and thyme and rosemary sprigs, and place filet in the pan for roughly 3 minutes or until a nice caramelization forms, then turn filet over and sauté for 3 minutes. Push the filet up against the sides of the pan so that the filet's sides are caramelized as well.

Add the unsalted butter and baste the filet with the melted butter over and over for 30 seconds. When filet is seared on all sides, remove from pan and let it rest. Remove the herb sprigs and garlic cloves and drain the butter from pan, discard, and place the pan back on the stove.

Add a tsp of olive oil to the heated pan, add cipollini onions and sauté for 2 minutes. Add the mushrooms, minced garlic, and minced shallots, and sauté for 1 minute. Deglaze with red wine, add green peppercorns, simmer until the pan is almost but not completely dry. Add the rich veal stock and simmer until liquid starts to coat the back of a spoon. Whisk in soft fresh butter, place filet back in the pan and baste.

Adjust seasoning. Ready to serve.

frisée salad with macadamia nuts, poached egg, and truffle oil

Yields 1 salad

Salad:

- 2–3 small heads of frisée greens, washed and dried
- 10 haricots verts, blanched and shocked
- 2 strips cooked smoked bacon, large dice
- 10 macadamia nuts, toasted and cut in halves
- 8 focaccia croutons
- ¼ cup crumbled bleu cheese
- 1 tsp shallots, minced
- 2 tsp chives, sliced fine
- truffle oil (drizzle)
- 1 poached egg
- poaching liquid: water, kosher salt, squeeze of lemon

Dressing:

- 3 Tbsp olive oil
- 2 cloves crushed garlic
- 1 Tbsp sherry vinegar
- kosher salt, fresh cracked pepper

Wash greens in cold water and dry with clean side towel.

Fill an 8-inch sauté pan ¾ full of water, squeeze ¼ lemon and 2 tsp of kosher salt into the pan and bring to a simmer. Crack egg into pan and gently simmer until soft poach.

Preheat a separate sauté pan over medium heat, add olive oil. Sauté haricots verts and minced shallots until hot. In a bowl add the frisée, bacon, macadamia nuts, haricots verts, croutons, and bleu cheese; add the dressing and toss. Place in serving bowl, top off with poached egg, add snipped chive, and drizzle with truffle oil and fresh cracked pepper.

For the dressing: place the oil in a cup with garlic, a pinch of fresh cracked pepper and kosher salt, and microwave 30 seconds, remove and whisk in sherry vinegar.

chicken soup with cilantro and a squeeze of lime

Yields 10 portions

1 small celery stalk, cleaned and medium dice
2 carrots, peeled and medium dice
1 onion, peeled and medium dice
2 tsp thyme, chopped fine
1 tsp rosemary, chopped fine
1 Tbsp garlic, minced
¼ cup cilantro, chopped
3 qt chicken stock
2 6 oz boneless chicken breast
1 lime

In a pot over medium heat, bring 1 quart of chicken stock to a simmer, add chicken breasts into the simmering stock. Poach the chicken for 15–20 min, or until cooked through. Remove chicken from stock and set aside to cool. Once cooled, medium dice the chicken and set aside.

In a separate pot over medium-high heat, sweat the onion, carrots, and celery, being careful not to caramelize. Add thyme, garlic, and rosemary and stir for 1 minute. Add 2 quarts of chicken stock. Let simmer for 5 minutes. Add your diced chicken.

Once chicken is warmed through, turn off the stove and serve soup into bowls. Add a pinch of fresh cilantro and finish with a squeeze of lime.

grilled brie and truffle crab sandwich

Yields 1 sandwich

  2 slices of brioche bread
4–6 thin slices of cucumber
  4 slices of brie
  2 oz lump crab meat
4–5 thin slices of truffle (fresh or canned)
  1 Tbsp unsalted butter
  1 Tbsp dill, freshly chopped
  ¼ lemon
  1 Tbsp mayonnaise
     salt and pepper (to taste)
     cayenne (to taste)
     truffle oil

In a small bowl, season crab with salt and pepper and a touch of cayenne. Add a squeeze of lemon, freshly chopped dill, and mayonnaise. Mix until well incorporated.

Lay one slice of brioche bread down, top with the crab mixture, then with cucumber slices, brie cheese slices, and truffle slices. For extra truffle flavor, drizzle with truffle oil. Top with the other slice of bread.

In a medium-high skillet, melt butter and lay sandwich in the pan, toast for about 2 minutes on each side (until a nice golden brown and the inside is warm and melted).

Cut sandwich, cutting off crusts if desired, and serve.

new england omelet

Yields 1 omelet

3 eggs

1 Tbsp water

2 Tbsp olive oil (or any type of vegetable oil will suffice)

⅓ cup sweet onion, thinly sliced

⅓ cup green apple, thinly sliced

1 scallion, sliced

⅓ cup cheddar cheese, grated

In a medium-size pan on medium heat, add 1 Tbsp of oil and sauté the sliced onions until golden brown. Once done, set to the side.

In a separate bowl, crack the eggs, add water, and whisk until
well mixed. Heat a medium-sized non-stick pan on a medium-
low temperature and add 1 Tbsp of oil. When the butter in the
pan is melted and bubbly, pour in the eggs. Don't stir! Add the
onions and about half of the grated cheddar. Let the eggs cook for
up to a minute or until the bottom starts to set.

With a heat-resistant rubber spatula, gently push one edge of
the egg into the center of the pan, while tilting the pan to allow
the liquid egg on top to flow underneath. Repeat this until there's
no liquid left.

Your egg mixture should easily slide around on the nonstick
surface. If it sticks at all, loosen it with your spatula.

Now gently flip the egg pancake over, using your spatula to
ease it over if necessary. Cook for another few seconds, or until
there is no uncooked egg left.

Add the apple slices in the middle. Fold the omelet in half and
top with more cheese and a sprinkle of scallions.

Move the omelet from the pan to a plate and serve.

chicken stock

Yields 1 gallon

 3 lbs chicken bones
 1 lb onion, rough chopped
 ½ lb carrots, washed and rough chopped
 ½ lb celery, washed and rough chopped
 5 garlic cloves, peeled and crushed
 5 bay leaves
15 peppercorns
1½ gal water
    olive oil

In a large pot, on medium-high heat, add the oil and vegetables and sweat (no caramelizing) for 3 minutes. Add chicken bones and stir around in the pot. Add garlic, bay leaves, and peppercorns, sweat for 2 more minutes. Add the water, enough to just cover the bones.

Let simmer for 1 hour. Be careful to not let it boil. Skim fat off the top every so often.

Strain and cool.

chef's "landreaux special" chicken and white bean soup

Yields 10 portions

1 Tbsp olive oil
2 shallots, small dice
½ tsp salt
1 pinch pepper
1 cup spicy chorizo sausage
4 cloves garlic
¼ cup dry white wine
7 cups chicken stock
1 cup cannellini beans, drained and rinsed
1 bunch escarole, stalks removed, leaves chopped
2 cups cooked chicken, medium dice
   Parmesan cheese, shaved

Heat the olive oil in a 4-quart pot over medium-high heat. Add shallots, salt and pepper, and cook for 3 minutes or until shallots are soft. Add the chorizo and sauté until lightly brown, add the garlic and cook for 2 more minutes until fragrant. Add the wine and simmer for 1–2 minutes.

Pour in the chicken stock and bring to a boil. Add the beans and escarole. Simmer for 5 more minutes, or until heated through and the broth has thickened. Add the cooked chicken. Simmer for 4–5 minutes.

Portion into soup cups and sprinkle with Parmesan cheese.

chicken consommé

Yields 16 portions

1   lb ground chicken meat
1   lb mirepoix:
      1 carrot, small dice
      ½ onion, small dice
      1 celery stalk, small dice
      ½ leek stalk, washed and small dice
      5–6 button mushrooms, small dice
      1 cup rutabaga, small dice
1   gal chicken stock
4   egg whites
2   bay leaves
3   whole cloves
10 black peppercorns
2   tsp lemon juice
1   Tbsp dry white wine
2   garlic cloves, finely chopped
1   Tbsp thyme, roughly chopped

In a medium sized mixing bowl, combine meat, mirepoix, and all ingredients except for the stock, forming a raft. In a medium-large pot, add chicken stock. Add the raft to the stock, mixing in completely.

Turn on medium-high heat and using a thermometer, bring the mixture to 120°F, stirring frequently. Adjust to medium-low heat.

Once mixture has reached 120°F, stop stirring, and let the raft rise and clear the stock. Never allow the stock to boil!

Simmer the stock ever so slightly until clear, about 40 minutes, and then strain the liquid through a cheese cloth and strainer. Adjust seasoning and serve.

prime rib

Yields: 16 slices

1 prime rib, boneless
1 cup your favorite steak seasoning (or kosher salt and fresh
   cracked pepper, in a ratio of roughly 3:1)
¼ cup olive oil

Let prime rib sit at room temperature for 30 minutes. Combine steak seasoning and oil to make a paste. Rub the paste all over the prime rib, massaging it into the meat.

Pre-heat the oven to 425°F. Roast the prime rib for 30 minutes at this temperature to create a nice crust.

Bring the temperature down to 300°F and slow-cook the prime rib until it reaches an internal temperature of 120°F (medium rare). Check internal temperature using a meat thermometer. This should take about 4–5 hours. If you prefer more well done, cook to an internal temperature of 135°F (about 5–6 hours).

Remove the meat from the oven, cover with aluminum foil, and let it sit for about 25 minutes.

Slice into 1-inch thick slices and serve.

owen's favorite hot chocolate

Yields: 4 servings

  2 cups evaporated milk
  ½ cup whole milk
  1 whole vanilla bean
  ¼ cup sugar
  1 Tbsp unsweetened cocoa
1½ tsp ground cinnamon
  ¼ tsp ancho chili powder
  1 dried red chili
  6 cinnamon sticks
1½ oz bittersweet chocolate, broken into pieces
  ¼ cup heavy whipping cream

In a heavy saucepan, whisk evaporated milk, whole milk, sugar, cocoa, 1 tsp of cinnamon, chili powder, and vanilla bean (cut in half lengthwise and scrape the vanilla beans into the pan, leaving a little bit to the side for the whipped cream). Add 2 of the cinnamon sticks and the dried red chili and cook gently over medium-low heat until warm (not boiling!).

Add chocolate pieces and cook, whisking until melted. Gently bring to a low boil, then reduce heat and simmer on low for 10 minutes, until liquid thickens, whisking often.

In a stand mixer, combine heavy whipping cream with the rest of the cinnamon and a little vanilla and sugar to sweeten. Beat with whisk attachment until peaks form.

Ladle hot cocoa into your mug of choice, top with whipped cream, and garnish with a cinnamon stick.

bruschetta with tomato, fresh mozzarella, and fresh basil

Yields 8 slices

8 slices French baguette, about ¾ inch thick
1 lb mozzarella, sliced
4 plum tomatoes, medium diced (seeds removed)
1 onion, medium diced
½ cup unsalted butter, softened to room temperature
4–5 basil leaves, freshly chopped
    olive oil (to taste)
    reduced balsamic ("balsamic glaze") (to taste)
    cracked black pepper (to taste)

Slice baguette into 8 three-quarter-inch slices. Slather each baguette slice with butter and in a skillet on medium heat, toast each side of the slices until golden brown in color. Set aside.

In a separate skillet, heat olive oil on medium-high heat. Add diced onions and sweat until transparent. Add diced tomatoes and a little fresh cracked black pepper. Sauté for 2 minutes. Fold in freshly chopped basil.

Spoon tomato mixture on each toasted slice. Sprinkle a little more olive oil on top, then drizzle reduced balsamic and top with a slice of mozzarella.

Toast in oven at 325°F until cheese is fully melted, but not brown. Remove from oven and finish with reduced balsamic and cracked black pepper.

Serve and enjoy.

chicken consommé with parisienne vegetables

Yields 16 portions

1 recipe of chicken consommé (above)
1 qt chicken stock
3 cups ice water
3 large zucchini
3 large yellow summer squash
1 butternut squash, peeled
1 black trumpet mushroom, chiffonade cut (finely sliced)
¼ cup micro celery

To Parisienne the zucchini and squashes: press the open side of a small melon baller against the vegetable and rock it side to side, with pressure, to cut into the vegetable. Once it is pushed in as far as it can go, scoop out the little ball. Repeat until you have 48 zucchini balls, 48 butternut squash balls, and 48 yellow summer squash balls. Keep each vegetable separate.

In a pot over medium heat, bring chicken stock to a simmer. Add the summer squash and blanch till tender, then remove and place in ice water to stop the cooking process. Set to the side. Repeat for the butternut squash and zucchini.

In a separate pot, bring chicken consommé to a simmer.

Portion out your Parisienne vegetables, 9 per bowl (3 butternut, 3 zucchini, 3 yellow squash). Top with a pinch of chiffonade black trumpet mushrooms.

When ready to serve, ladle the heated consommé into each bowl evenly. Finish with a plouche of micro celery.

Serve and enjoy.

frisée salad with goat cheese, apple, pears, smoked bacon and candied pecans

Yields 4 entrée salads

Salad:

- 1 head frisée, cleaned and lightly chopped
- 1 bunch watercress, ends cut
- 1 bunch arugula
- 2 cups spinach, stems picked off
- ½ cup goat cheese crumbles
- 1 apple, julienned
- 1 bosc pear, julienned
- 4 slices of smoked bacon, diced
- ¼ cup candied pecans

Dressing:

- 2 Tbsp champagne vinegar
- 2 Tbsp white balsamic vinegar
- ¾ cup olive oil
- 1 Tbsp parsley, freshly picked and lightly chopped
- 1 tsp thyme, freshly picked and lightly chopped
- 1 Tbsp chives, freshly picked and lightly chopped
- 1 Tbsp honey
- 1 tsp Dijon mustard
  salt and pepper to taste

In a mixing bowl whisk both vinegars, oil, herbs, honey, mustard, and salt and pepper until combined.

In a pan on medium-high heat, cook smoked bacon to desired crispiness.

Clean and dry all greens. In a large bowl, toss together with julienned apples and pears and ½ cup of the dressing. Divide greens into 4 serving bowls and top with goat cheese, bacon, and candied pecans.

Drizzle remaining dressing over the salads and serve.

chive, parsnip and potato purée

Yields 2 portions

2 parsnips, peeled and large dice
¼ cup onion, large dice
2 cloves of garlic
1 Tbsp olive oil
¼ cup dry white wine
1 cup whole milk
1 potato, peeled and quartered
1 Tbsp unsalted butter
 salt and pepper to taste
1 Tbsp chives, snipped

In a sauté pan on medium heat, add oil, parsnip, onion, and garlic and sweat for 5–7 minutes. Add white wine and reduce until dry. Add the whole milk and cook until tender. Once done, strain out parsnips, onion, and garlic from the pan, saving the milk.

In a separate pot, add potato and fill with enough salted water to cover. Place on stove, turn on heat and bring to a simmer, cook until tender. Once done, drain the water from the pot. Place the potatoes back on the stove with low heat for 2 minutes until dry.

In a food mill, rice the potatoes and parsnip-onion mixture together.

In a blender, combine riced vegetables with butter and ½ cup of the reserved milk and pulse until smooth, adding more reserved milk as needed (texture should be slightly thinner than mashed potatoes). Pour purée into a bowl and fold in snipped chives. Serve and enjoy.

Note: Do not over-blend or the mixture will become too starchy.

charbroiled prime filet of beef tenderloin with oyster mushrooms and bordelaise sauce

Yields 1 serving

- 1　6-oz prime filet of beef tenderloin
- 6　small oyster mushrooms, trimmed and brushed clean of soil
- 3　small cipollini onions, peeled and quartered
- ¼　cup leeks, medium dice
- 1　tsp garlic, minced
- 1　tsp shallots, minced
- 1　sprig rosemary
- 1　sprig thyme
- 2　cloves garlic, whole, peeled
- 1　Tbsp tomato paste
- ¼　cup Burgundy wine
- ¼　cup rich veal stock (demi-glace)

- 2　Tbsp unsalted butter for filet baste
- 　　olive oil
- 　　kosher salt and fresh ground pepper
- 1　Tbsp unsalted butter to finish the sauce

Let filet sit at room temperature for 30 minutes. Season with fresh ground pepper and kosher salt and drizzle with a teaspoon of olive oil.

Preheat sauté pan on medium heat. Pour 2 tsp of olive oil into the base of the pan, add garlic cloves and thyme and rosemary sprigs, and place filet in the pan for roughly 3 minutes or until a nice caramelization forms, then turn filet over and sauté the other side for 3 minutes. Push the filet up against the sides of the pan so that the filet's sides are caramelized as well.

Add the unsalted butter and baste the filet with the melted butter over and over for 30 seconds. When filet is seared on all sides, remove from pan and let it rest. Remove the herb sprigs and garlic cloves and drain the butter from pan, discard, and place the pan back on the stove.

Preheat oven to 375°F. Coat onions, leeks, and mushrooms with olive oil, salt and pepper, and lay flat in a roasting pan. Roast for about 10 minutes or until tender. Remove pan from oven and put on the stove at a medium-high heat. Add tomato paste into the pan and incorporate into the veggies. Deglaze with the Burgundy and simmer until the pan is almost but not completely dry. Add the rich veal stock and simmer until liquid starts to coat the back of a spoon. Whisk in soft fresh butter, place filet back in pan, and baste. Adjust seasoning.

Place filet on the plate, then spoon a little sauce over top and the rest artistically around the plate. Ready to serve.

broccolini, roasted cipollini, and baby carrots

Yields 5 portions

 1 bunch broccolini
10 cipollini onions (small), peeled
 5 baby carrots, halved
 3 Tbsp olive oil
½ cup Madeira wine
 1 Tbsp unsalted butter
    salt, pepper, sugar to taste

Carrots: Toss carrots in 1 Tbsp of olive oil, salt and pepper, and a touch of sugar. In a roasting pan, roast in the oven at 375°F for about 15 minutes or until tender.

Broccolini: Trim one inch off the stem. Bring a pot of salted water to a light simmer and blanch the broccolini until just tender. Remove from hot water and set the broccolini in ice water to stop the cooking process. Remove from ice water once cooled and set aside. When ready to serve, melt butter in a sauté pan and sauté the broccolini in the butter until warmed through.

Cipollini: Heat 1 Tbsp of oil in a large sauce pan over medium-high heat. Heavily sear one side of the cipollini, then the other side. Add the Madeira and reduce by half. Finish by whisking in butter and season with salt and pepper.

Toss carrots and cipollini together. Place broccolini on plates, then spoon carrots and cipollini over the stems.

chef thomas's famous oat blueberry pancakes

Yields about 8 pancakes

  1 cup oat flour
2½ tsp baking powder
  ½ tsp salt
  1 large egg, beaten
  1 cup milk or water
  1 tsp raw honey
  1 Tbsp vegetable oil
  1 cup fresh blueberries

Stir together dry ingredients, pressing out any lumps. In a seperate bowl, blend egg and other liquid ingredients together; beat well. Add to dry ingredients; mix well. Add blueberries and mix gently.

Drop by tablespoons onto a hot oiled griddle. Turn each pancake once, when air bubbles start to appear.

Place the hot pancakes on your serving plates, with butter and pure maple syrup.

Place a single flower in a one-stem vase.

Now go serve it to someone you love.

To see Chef Carroll demonstrate and discuss a selection of recipes from the book, visit TheIngredientsofGreatness.com.

the story behind the story

In 2009 John got an email out of the blue from a chef he'd never met from halfway across the country. Charles loved John's book *The Go-Giver* and had been using it with his staff at the River Oaks Country Club in Houston. As Charles says, "It's funny how a dream can take shape by blindly emailing one of your favorite authors—and having him actually respond!"

The Club brought John out to Houston to speak about *The Go-Giver*, and Charles told John about his idea for a story about a young man in trouble, who learns life lessons in a cramped diner kitchen from a crusty old retired chef. They talked about it into the night, and the next day. And kept talking about it.

Eight years later, here it is.

While *The Recipe* is fiction, it is inspired by and draws upon quite a few elements from Charles's own life. All those awards on the Chef's home office walls—the Olympic gold medals (and that first early bronze, too), the White House photos with presidents, the public service (though for Charles it was serving U.S. troops in Afghanistan, not a flood-ravaged town in the midwest)—that's all Charles. The old corner brownstone diner is real, too; it was called the Mapletown Dinette, in St. Johnsbury, Vermont, and Charles's father owned and ran it. Charles still remembers running up and down the counter aisle, trying to get all those stools spinning at once. And Charles's dad was a culinary instructor at St. Johnsbury Academy, where Charles says he learned critical early lessons of discipline and respect. There really was a Ruth (Charles's mom) and a Bernie (her sister), and later on, when Charles served as executive chef at the Balsams Grand Resort, he had an amazing breakfast cook whom everyone called Mad Dog. There was a real Chef Kellaway, too—an instructor at the Culinary Institute of America who influenced Charles's Olympic ambitions.

When Charles was about Owen's age, his dad was named state president of the Elks Club, and he put Charles in charge of preparing the banquet held in his honor, much like Owen and the banquet in chapter 14.

"Chef Kellaway's Rules of the Kitchen" take their inspiration from the "20 Guiding Principles" Charles uses in his kitchen today. (And yes, every employee carries them on a little laminated card in his or her pocket.)

Not that you'd want to take these parallels too far. The core story here *is* fiction, after all. Charles did not lose his father at age fourteen, did not throw a rock through a warehouse window, and was not the troubled kid of the story.

Interestingly, though, there are quite a few well-known chefs who *did* have exactly those kinds of rough childhoods, and far worse, and whose lives have been turned around and given a fresh start in the environment of the kitchen. There's something about the discipline of cooking that has the potential to heal the soul, even as it disciplines the mind and body. Chef Charles has worked with a lot of kids like that, and still does today.

For a video interview with the authors on The Story Behind the Story, visit TheIngredientsofGreatness.com.

acknowledgments

Build your team; that's the Chef's Rule Five, and was Coach Devon's cardinal rule, too. Those two knew what they were talking about. Great cooking is never a solo enterprise; there is always an unseen army of sous chefs, assistants, teachers, mentors, suppliers, farmers, and a thousand others who patiently grew, nurtured, and prepared everything you're seeing and tasting on your plate—people who make the chef look good in the process.

A story is no different from a meal: its sources and ingredients come from far and wide. Our deepest thanks go out:

To our early readers, who came back with generous helpings of enormously valuable critique that helped us bring out the story's true flavors: Faye Atchison, Dan Clements, Barbara Engberg, Robert Gehorsam, Margaret Hanratty, James Justice, Ana Gabriel Mann, Margret McBride, Abbie McClung, Patricia Petty-Munns, Dondi Scumaci, Randy Stelter, and John Stetler.

To Jessica Cowan, who started working at River Oaks Country Club directly out of culinary school and has grown into an amazing assistant who manages all Chef Charles's crazy ideas; we are blessed by her talent and dedication. To Bob Burg, Dan Clements, and Laura Steward, for their friendship and boundless generosity; to Tim Grahl and Jane Friedman, for their wisdom and expertise; and to Hannah Ineson, for the beautifully executed cover illustration.

from Charles:

To my coauthor, John David Mann; thank you, John, for answering that email from a total stranger! I am humbled to have the opportunity to work with you, and creating this project together has been a true pleasure for me.

To my mom and dad for instilling in me that "chewing off the end of the table" work ethic, passion, and drive the Chef talks about. Dad made the best fresh-baked bread you can imagine; I can still smell the loaves coming out of the oven, and I'll never forget watching him bake all those pastries by hand, including the donuts and Danishes, bear claws and (my favorite) bird's nests. My dad passed away while this project was still in its early stages, but I'm grateful that my mom had the chance to read most of this book prior to her passing. I'll never forget the image of her magnifying glass resting on the manuscript, lying on the coffee table and opened to the last five pages. Mom, you were always my rock and my biggest supporter.

To all my dear friends, competitors, and coaches, and everyone throughout my career who has given me a chance and supported me with all my dreams and crazy projects—and especially those who told me that some of my dreams were impossible: you have been my biggest inspiration.

To my wife, Torill, who constantly finds the patience to support me in everything I do; and to my two children, Kelsey and Randi: you have taken your fair share of backseats to all my ambitions and are both extremely successful in your own right; you two are the most amazing kids a father could hope for.

from John:

To my coauthor, Chef Charles Carroll: when you approached me
with the idea for this book, I fell in love right then and there with
Owen and his story, and with the idea of weaving a coming-of-age
parable around life lessons in the kitchen. I've always adored food
and cooking, and in the course of conceiving, drafting, and writing
this story, I had the chance to try out every technique and every
recipe (plus many more besides!) and refine my own kitchen skills.

To my parents, Alfred and Carolyn Mann, who taught me all
about great music, great writing, and great food, and that they all
are woven from the same threads.

To all the teachers, colleagues, and friends who have helped
elucidate and articulate the ingredients of greatness.

And to my sweet wife (and incomparable cook), Ana Gabriel
Mann, for your famous (in this house, at least) oat and blueberry
pancake recipe, and even more for being the secret ingredient in
every recipe I make. As I said in my wedding vows, "I love to cook
with you . . ."—and I look forward to years and years of days and
nights filled with great food and even greater companionship.

about the authors

CHEF CHARLES CARROLL (chefcharlescarroll.com) is an eight-time Culinary Olympian who travels the world speaking on championship thinking and personal greatness. Chef Carroll won his first Culinary Olympics gold medal at the 1988 games at the age of 24 (the youngest member of the team) and has since participated in the quadrennial Olympics as team member, coach, and judge. He was named one of the year's Great Country Inn Chefs by the James Beard Foundation (1993) and is past president of the World Association of Chefs Societies, with over 10 million members in 105 countries. Among his titles and distinctions, Chef Carroll has been inducted into the World Master Chefs Association, the American Academy of Chefs, the Confrérie de la Chaîne des Rôtisseurs, and the Honorable Order of the Golden Toque.

For his work with U.S. troops abroad, Chef Carroll was personally commended by U.S. presidents Jimmy Carter, George H.W. Bush, Bill Clinton, George W. Bush, and Barack Obama. In 2013 he was awarded the Honorable Order of Saint Martin by the U.S. Army. Chef Carroll currently serves as Executive Chef of Houston's River Oaks Country Club.

JOHN DAVID MANN (johndavidmann.com) performed his first composition, a musical score for Aeschylus's *Prometheus Bound*, in Greece at the play's original venue when he was 13, and won the BMI Awards for Student Composers at 15. At 17 he spearheaded a group of students who started their own high school, and after graduating the following year joined the faculty. He performed as a concert cellist before turning to careers as an entrepreneur and an author.

John is coauthor of the bestselling classic *The Go-Giver: A Little Story About a Powerful Business Idea*, which has sold more than half a million copies in more than two dozen languages. Winner of the 2008 Axiom Business Book Award's Gold Medal and the 2017 Living Now Book Award's Evergreen Medal for its "contributions to positive global change," *The Go-Giver* was hailed as "the most important parable about business—and life—of our time" by bestselling author and Wharton professor Adam Grant; "a small book that packs a huge idea" by bestselling author Daniel Pink; "a good description of many of the most amazing people I've encountered" by Arianna Huffington; and "a must-read by anyone who wants to change the world" by talk show host Glenn Beck. *Inc.* magazine named it one of the 18 Most Motivational Books of All Time.

His other titles include the *New York Times* bestsellers *Flash Foresight* (with Daniel Burrus) and *The Red Circle* (with Brandon Webb) and the national bestsellers *Among Heroes* (with Brandon Webb), *The Slight Edge* (with Jeff Olson), and *Real Leadership* (with John Addison). His 2011 *Take the Lead* (with Betsy Myers) was named by Tom Peters and the *Washington Post* as Best Leadership Book of 2011.

CPSIA information can be obtained
at www.ICGtesting.com
Printed in the USA
LVOW11*1203251017
553707LV00004B/24/P